IT MUST BE LOVE

Children's entertainer Brianna Madison is on the brink of setting up a clown school. She just needs to locate suitable premises — and handsome Nathan Telford might have the answer. Nathan has never met anyone quite like this particular clown before. Everywhere she goes, disaster quickly follows. Even as he realises he can't stop thinking about her, he is fully aware that she will bring chaos into his well-ordered life — and that is something he definitely doesn't need . . .

Books by Suzanne Ross Jones
in the Linford Romance Library:

YOUR SECRET SMILE
IT HAD TO BE YOU
SEE YOU IN MY DREAMS
EMBRACEABLE YOU

SUZANNE ROSS JONES

IT MUST BE LOVE

Complete and Unabridged

LINFORD
Leicester

First published in Great Britain in 2016

First Linford Edition
published 2017

A catalogue record for this book is available
from the British Library.

ISBN 978–1–4448–3184–9

Published by
F. A. Thorpe (Publishing)
Anstey, Leicestershire

Set by Words & Graphics Ltd.
Anstey, Leicestershire
Printed and bound in Great Britain by
T. J. International Ltd., Padstow, Cornwall

This book is printed on acid-free paper

1

A Lift Home

'This really is very kind of you.'

Nathan Telford glanced wryly at the breathless clown cluttering the interior of his car and raised an eyebrow. 'Kind' hardly came into it. It was practical, nothing more. Without replying, he fired the ignition, and his Aston Martin roared to life.

'I need to be back by four, and I'd have felt horribly guilty if I'd taken Claire or Simon away from their daughter's party.' She paused briefly, presumably to take a breath. 'My car's given up the ghost — Simon already had to collect me this morning.'

She was a chatterbox. Of course she was. Nathan's grip tightened on the steering wheel. Claire owed him big-time for this. But he supposed even acting as chauffeur to a clown was infinitely preferable to being monopolised by his sister's scary friend.

He shuddered and wondered what his sister had said about him that made Adrianne feel she had the right to corner him as she had — and at a children's party of all places.

Thank goodness Claire had needed him to drive the clown home. It had been a fair trade — a lift in exchange for an early exit from his niece's fifth birthday party.

'My Aunt Zoe is horrified I drive around in something so unreliable, but I really like it — it's quirky and colourful, and exactly the kind of car you'd expect a clown to drive.'

Horrified by the very thought of a clown car, he tried to tune out the clown's chatter.

If he was honest, he knew he shouldn't have been so keen to leave the party. He loved his family, of course he did, but a noisy group of children was *so* not his thing. And when you added Claire's predatory friend into the mix, it became Nathan's idea of a nightmare.

With a sense of relief, he steered the car down the vast expanse of his sister's driveway and swept out onto the road.

'I will get home by four, won't I?' Madison Clown's anxious question brought his attention back to her. There was no doubt from her tone that being home by four was important to her. She would be frowning, he was sure, if she'd been able to manage any facial mobility under the weight of her make-up.

'We'll be cutting it fine,' he replied calmly. 'But it's doable as long we don't get caught in traffic.'

'Good.' She relaxed back against the headrest, the wild orange curls of her clown wig bouncing distractingly in the periphery of his vision.

He wished she'd changed out of her costume, instead of marring the pristine leather upholstery with her jumble of bright colours. Her insistence on getting home by her deadline, though, had urged him to suggest that perhaps leaving immediately might be the brightest option.

3

Not such a bad thing when it achieved two aims with one hit. Safe delivery of the clown to her home in good time for whatever she had arranged for four o'clock this afternoon. And getting himself the heck out of the party.

He still didn't know why Claire couldn't have found herself a local clown. Despite his sister's insistence that Madison Clown was the best in the business, Nathan seriously doubted any children's entertainer could be worth this much trouble.

'What sort of person becomes a clown, anyway?' He heard a sharp intake of breath and realised he'd spoken aloud. He winced. It wasn't like him to be so tactless. He risked a quick glance across and met with a pair of amused brown eyes.

'What sort of person attends a five-year-old's birthday party in a business suit?'

She was laughing at him, no doubt about that, but Nathan reckoned that had to be the least he deserved. 'I came from the office.'

'On a Saturday?'

He shrugged. 'People work at weekends. You're working yourself.'

'That's different. And you know it.'

They were on the motorway now and, worryingly, the clown seemed to be performing some sort of striptease in his passenger seat — shedding one colourful scrap of material after another into the bag wedged in at her feet.

He cleared his throat. 'What are you doing?'

'Getting changed.'

'In the car?'

'I have a meeting at four. I can't possibly turn up looking like this. It wouldn't be seemly.'

Unbelievable. 'And getting undressed in the car *is?*'

'I've no choice.'

In an attempt to remove her trousers in the limited space, she raised a leg at an impossible angle. Nathan did his best to keep his attention on the road. He still remembered the demonstration he'd been treated to earlier, as her agile and flexible body had performed sundry gymnastics. Some of her somersaults had defied gravity.

As though to confirm his views on the inappropriateness of the situation, a lorry sounded its horn — just as Madison wriggled out her overly large purple with orange spots trousers to reveal a pair of endless legs in tiny denim cut-offs.

He wanted to make a clever remark about hot pants being so much more suitable for a meeting than a clown costume, but he reckoned that would be one step too far across the rudeness line.

Even though he did his best to keep his eyes fixed firmly on the road ahead, Nathan could sense her movements. And it was amazing what you could see out of the corner of your eye — even when you weren't trying to look.

He reached up and loosened the knot of his tie a little as she pulled her matching clown top over her head to reveal a tiny black vest.

'That's better,' she sighed. 'My

costume's much too hot for this time of year.' The wig followed the clothing into the bag. 'As is the hair.'

Not his type, he told himself. Just as he wasn't interested in aggressive older women like Adrianne, he also didn't dally with flighty clowns. Nathan's girlfriends dressed conservatively and behaved with decorum and they didn't wear a ragbag of mad colours and do back flips and magic tricks for a living.

She took a handful of wipes from her bag and began the job of restoring her face to normality.

He risked another glance. Her wide mouth and broad smile had him wondering briefly why she bothered with the painted clown smile. And then she pulled the pins out of her hair and a riot of toffee-coloured curls tumbled over her creamy shoulders. She didn't need to bother with the wig either, when she possessed a natural version so much wilder than the artificial.

'Who are you meeting at four?' It didn't matter to him — he was only making

7

conversation, but he couldn't get it out of his head she might be taking those endless legs to meet up with a boyfriend.

She rummaged in her bag and emerged triumphant with a pair of flat heeled strappy sandals that she slipped onto her feet.

'Letting agent,' she replied cheerfully.

'You're looking to make a move?'

'I'm looking for business premises.'

Interest immediately captured, he glanced over again. Perhaps she had hidden depths. 'What line of business are you in?'

'I'm going to set up a clown school,' she replied, the seriousness of her tone at odds with her words.

Nathan hadn't even been aware clowns went to school. He glanced quickly in his mirrors before indicating and moving into the outside lane.

She was so not his type.

★ ★ ★

Madison sat back in the soft leather seat with a loud sigh and glanced over at her reluctant chauffeur from beneath her lashes. Serious didn't begin to cover

8

Nathan Telford's demeanour. He'd barely cracked a smile since he'd turned up at his niece's birthday party. And he definitely resented that he'd drawn the short straw to take her home.

She couldn't understand it. According to his sister he lived in London, she wasn't even taking him out of his way. Not much out of his way, in any case.

Gorgeous, though, she acknowledged, risking another furtive glance. In fact, he was punch you in the gut attractive — in a traditional business tycoon sort of way — with his hard jaw, straight nose and those blue, blue eyes.

If you liked that sort of thing.

Which she didn't. Not really. He might have been lovely to look at, he was also far too severe and self-controlled for her tastes. Far, far too grumpy.

Not only was his dark blond hair way too short, but he'd worn a suit and tie to his five- year-old niece's birthday party — and on one of the hottest days of the year, too. Even now, when he'd removed his navy jacket, he sat aloof and pristine in his crisp white shirt and navy-blue silk tie.

It would be obvious to anyone he was buttoned up tight.

Besides, even if he had been to her taste, he was so out of her league there was no point even dreaming. His car probably cost more than her entire flat. And, having seen the country house where his sister lived, it was obvious the whole family was loaded. In her experience, when rich people like Nathan mixed with ordinary people like her, it always ended badly.

She turned her attention to the road, aware that however easy he was to look at, she maybe shouldn't be staring. The view out of the window was just as disturbing, if for a different reason.

'The traffic's getting bad.' She tried to project calm, but she knew she sounded worried.

'We'll make it.' His voice sent unwelcome shivers down her spine. 'As long as it doesn't get any worse.'

'I really shouldn't have accepted the job today. Not when it was so far away and I'd already arranged to see this property.'

She'd been searching for somewhere to set up her school for ages. Everywhere she'd looked at had either been too small, or too expensive, or both. But this had sounded like it just might be perfect — a share of an industrial unit, the other half of which was being used as a dance studio. Although the agent had warned her there were several parties already interested, so she needed to move fast.

'It's so important I'm there promptly.'

Nathan's eyes were narrowed as he glanced across. 'As a matter of interest, why did you accept the booking for Daisy's party if you had plans for this afternoon?'

'I wasn't going to, but your sister can be very persuasive.' She had a feeling he already knew that — why else would he be driving her home when he so obviously didn't want to. 'If Claire hadn't pleaded, offered much more money than any clown had a right to expect, I'd be safely at home now, getting ready to go off to see the property.'

The temptation had been too much,

11

especially when the job would give her funds the boost they needed now she teetered on the brink of setting up her business. And, of course, Claire had played her winning hand and mentioned her daughter — and Madison hated to disappoint a child.

'Traffic just got worse,' he needlessly informed her as he pulled up at the tail end of a traffic jam.

'Oh no.' She could feel her dream slipping away and was powerless to do anything about it. 'Can't you get us out of this?' she pleaded helplessly.

'What do you suggest I do?'

'I don't know. Something. Claire told me you were a problem solver — that you could do anything. I really have to get back.'

Nathan grimaced. 'Claire exaggerated. Little sisters have a habit of hero worshiping their brothers,' he informed her. 'And Claire's no exception.'

'I can't risk losing this property. You have to be able to do something.'

'As we're boxed in by several lanes of cars and the central reservation, I'm afraid there's really nothing I can do.'

'Nothing,' she echoed faintly and the reasonable part of her brain knew it was true.

His blue eyes crinkled as he grinned, flashing perfect white teeth and, despite her frustration at the situation, her stomach flipped. She thought she preferred him grumpy — much safer.

'Unless you want me to rip off my shirt to reveal my superhero costume and fly you out of here in my arms.'

Now that would be an original solution. He looked strong, his lines muscular where his shirt touched his body. The thought of spending even a moment in his arms had her heart racing.

Stop it, she warned herself. *You know what happens when you fall for a man so far removed from your social circle.*

It was impossible to ignore the fact he was filthy rich. His very demeanour screamed breeding and the kind of self-assurance only possessed by those who had been wealthy since birth. She wouldn't be surprised to find Nathan's

13

family tree documented all the way back for centuries.

And she …?

Well, she'd been raised by her lovely Aunt Zoe — with no recollection of her parents. And even her aunt had been too ill for much of the time to take care of a child. There had been nobody else, so Madison had ended up in care.

Yet, despite the differences between them, despite the fact she needed desperately to get home, the image of him ripping off his shirt and taking her in his arms had been firmly and disturbingly planted.

She closed her eyes and shook her head in an attempt to dislodge the picture.

'We'll have to sit it out. You can make another appointment to view.'

'I can't — there are other people already interested. This is a one chance opportunity. If I miss the appointment then someone else will snap it up.'

'I'm sure, if you put your mind to it, you could find any number of suitable properties to house your clown school.'

14

She zipped her lips tight shut. There spoke a man for whom money posed no problem. How could she begin to explain to him the challenges involved in finding suitable premises when you couldn't afford to pay the going rent?

She hadn't much cared for his dismissive tone as he spoke of her dream, either. But she'd come across the same attitude before and realised the best way to deal with it was to say nothing.

They sat in silence for a while, Madison resolutely staring through the windscreen at the stationery traffic — willing it to move — and refusing to look at him. But she could feel his eyes on her.

Eventually, he sighed. 'I'm sorry, Madison. I can see this is important to you.'

'It's not your fault,' she grudgingly acknowledged. 'I can't blame you for a traffic jam.'

'Madison Clown — not your real name, I take it?'

Despite herself, she smiled, and her amused glance clashed with deepest blue.

'It would be pretty odd if it were.'

'I'm trying to ask you what you're called,' he replied smoothly. 'I only know you as Madison Clown, but now you've stripped away your costume it doesn't suite you.'

'Brianna Madison,' she replied. Wondering if she should add that she hated her first name. 'But everyone calls me Madison. It makes life easier.'

The traffic inched forward with nowhere near enough speed to give her hope they'd make it back in time. Frustration and disappointment clawed at her. Over the year she'd been looking for a property, the agent had been very helpful, but he had a duty to get the best deal for the client. And as she wouldn't be there to meet him at four, she had to admit defeat.

'It probably wouldn't have been right anyway. Not going by the number of places I've already seen. And they did say it was a bit rundown — that's why it was affordable.' With a sigh, she rummaged in her bag and pulled out her mobile. The very least she could do was to let the agency know she wouldn't make it.

'Everything OK?' Nathan asked as she replaced the phone.

'Hunky dory. They've got a list of prospective clients as long as their arms and appointments booked every fifteen minutes from four — they'll rent the property in no time.'

The traffic began to move just as it was too late to make any difference and, in typical motorway fashion, there seemed to be no reason for the delay.

'I wonder what else will go wrong today,' she mused. He sent a quizzical look winging her way. 'Disasters happen in threes. Missing my appointment was number one, so now I'm holding my breath for the other two,' she elaborated.

He shook his head and Madison got the distinct impression he wasn't impressed by frivolities such as superstitions. 'Some might think the first disaster was your car breaking down.'

'That still leaves another disaster waiting to happen.'

When they eventually arrived back in

her area of town, they drove around a corner to the street where she lived and straight into mayhem. And she realised she should never have tempted fate by expecting anything else to go wrong.

Disaster number three surpassed anything she could have imagined. The road had been cordoned off. Police, ambulance, and fire brigade blocked the road.

'Wait here, I'll see what's going on,' Nathan told her.

Being ordered to stay behind would normally have had Madison chasing after him but, too shocked to do anything else, she sat now and waited as he spoke to the police. Moments later he returned to the car grim-faced.

'There's been a gas leak — your street's been evacuated. Everyone's at the local community centre, I'll drop you off there.'

It smacked a bit too much of insti-tutionalism for Madison's liking. She'd been there, slept in dorms, been herded like one of so many cattle. Even now, as a rational adult, the thought of being forced to stay in a shelter and being ordered around by officialdom filled her with horror. And no doubt it showed, because Nathan seemed to read her panic.

'What is it, Madison?' he asked, his voice so soft and caring he hardly seemed the same man who had laughed at her dreams such a short time ago.

She looked at him helplessly and shook her head. 'I can't — I just can't go to that place.'

He was quiet for a moment — he seemed to be weighing up the various options.

'Is there somewhere else you could go?' he eventually asked and she was relieved he hadn't tried to persuade her.

She quickly ran through the possibilities. There was her aunt, of course, but Zoe was away on a belated honeymoon — she wouldn't be back until late tomorrow night. And that left only one other possibility. 'My friend, Adam,' she decided and gave Nathan the address.

If nothing else, Adam would offer tea and sympathy — and a sofa for the night if needed.

They arrived at Adam's place and, still numb with shock, Madison retrieved her bag and got out of the car.

'Thanks for the lift,' she said, forcing her face into something she hoped might resemble a smile.

'No problem.' He grinned back, looking happier and more relaxed than she'd yet seen him. She suspected he was pleased to be rid of her.

Even through her uneasiness at being displaced from her home, that thought disturbed her.

Hoisting her bag onto her shoulder, she made her way up the path. The instant she rang the bell to Adam's house, she remembered he wasn't home this weekend. Her bag of clown paraphernalia dropped onto the doorstep and she sank down beside it before resting her forehead on her knees.

She really couldn't face the thought of going to the community centre to sit it out with everyone else. But, given her situation, what other choice did she have?

2

Escape to Nathan's

Nathan stopped the car at a set of traffic lights at the end of the road and glanced in his rear-view mirror. And there was the clown, sitting on the doorstep looking completely dejected.

It seemed her friend wasn't home. It really wasn't her day.

Nor his, he realised.

With a sigh, he reversed the length of the road and got out of his car.

'Disaster number four?' he called across.

She looked up and forced her wide mouth into a smile, but it didn't quite reach her eyes. He should walk away, he'd more than fulfilled the terms of his initial promise; he'd brought her back to London and she wasn't his problem any longer.

But how could he just leave her here? She looked as close to the edge as he'd ever seen another human being.

'I forgot he's away this weekend, with his girlfriend, Jen.'

'What are you going to do?'

She shrugged. 'I'll think of something. I always do.'

He took a step closer. Her choice of words gave the impression today wasn't unusual. Did disaster follow her around on a regular basis? He gave silent thanks for his own well-ordered life and for the fact Madison Clown would soon be out of it.

'I can't leave you here all weekend.'

'I'm hoping to go back to my own flat soon.' Her brow crinkled. 'I forgot to ask — did they say how long it would take to sort out the problem?'

He shrugged. 'Anything from a couple of hours to a day or two.'

She sighed noisily. 'I don't even have any money — your sister gave me a cheque and I never take my purse on jobs.'

'Get back in the car, Madison.'

She was appalled and it showed. 'I couldn't possibly. I've already put you to far too much trouble.'

'And I can't possibly leave you half dressed on your friend's doorstep.'

She glanced down at her outfit. 'What's wrong with what I'm wearing?'

'Nothing,' he agreed grudgingly. She looked gorgeous and that was part of the problem, the insubstantial outfit exposed far too much of her endlessly long legs. Really not the type of clothing suited to a night on the streets. 'But you'll get cold in shorts if you have to stay here all night.'

She nodded her agreement to that statement and he watched in fascination as her curls bobbed around her shoulders — almost as thought her hair had a life of its own.

'Come on,' he urged.

'No, thank you. I'll be fine.'

Nathan sighed. 'You don't want to go to the community centre. Your friend's away. You're camping out on a doorstep with only the clothes you're wearing and a clown outfit. You're kind of running out of options here.'

Her reluctance exasperated and intrigued him. As did his own eagerness to take her home. Nathan never encouraged visitors, even at the best of times — and this most definitely didn't resemble anything like the best of times.

It must be down to a misplaced sense of responsibility. Claire had asked him to bring Madison back to town and, until he deposited her either at her home or at another safe place, his job had not been completed.

'I'm not suggesting we spend the rest of our lives together,' he said, not prepared to give up. 'Just suggesting you sit this out at my place. You never know, you may be able to go home in a couple of hours.' He reached out a hand, but she didn't take it.

'I don't want to put you out.'

Much too late for that, but he controlled the urge to tell her so. He couldn't leave her in this situation, and alienating her now would only ensure they both spend the night on her friend's doorstep.

'You wouldn't be putting me out. All

you'll be doing is sitting out the wait in comfort. It won't be for long. They're trying to locate and contain the leak as we speak.'

As he watched, she sighed and the fight seemed to leave her.

There was unmistakeable hesitation as she reached out and finally took his hand. As their fingers met, awareness jolted through him.

Not stopping to think about it, he pulled her to her feet. She was tall. He hadn't realised just how tall — though her long legs should have maybe given him a hint. Even in her flat sandals, his eyes were level with the top of her toffee coloured curls — at six feet four that didn't normally happened, most of the women he dated barely reached his shoulders.

'Come on,' he said quietly. 'Let's go.'

He held her hand until he deposited her safely into the passenger seat.

He didn't examine too closely why he did that, either.

They drove through the streets in

silence. He didn't find it surprising she'd stopped chatting, given all she'd had to contend with today. Grudgingly, he admitted he missed the bubbly woman who'd been his constant companion for the past few hours.

Not that he'd admit that out loud, of course.

★ ★ ★

Madison didn't feel like talking. Complete mortification engulfed her. She knew Nathan felt obliged to offer her shelter and it horrified her. She'd rather take her chances on the streets than impose.

But as he'd refused to leave and the only alternative he'd been prepared to consider had been the community centre, she guessed his place had to be the lesser of the evils on offer to her.

Even though his wealth had been obvious from his clothes, car, and general demeanour, it was still a shock to see his penthouse. She'd never actually realised there were real people in the world who actually lived in places like this.

'There's so much room,' she said, almost to herself. 'And it's all so tidy.' It could almost be a show home.

He smiled, but didn't say anything.

The place was decidedly masculine, with lots of dark leather, and chrome, and wood. One complete wall of glass offered a magnificent view over the city skyline. It was breathtaking.

'Do you realise how lucky you are to live in a place like this?' She walked towards the window and admired the city skyline.

'It's got nothing to do with luck and everything to do with a healthy work ethic.'

Well, that told her. And she suspected he must believe it had nothing to do with his having been born privileged, either.

'But all this space ...' Perhaps, if she worked hard and took clowning to a new level, she too could live in a home like this. Or maybe not.

It suddenly occurred it was an awfully big space for one. Despite the manly look of the place, he might be married.

Disturbingly, the thought didn't make her happy.

'Do you live here alone?'

When he didn't answer immediately, she turned to look at him. He seemed surprised by her question.

'Yes.' His hard jaw clenched and his blue eyes narrowed. 'Why do you ask?'

She shrugged. 'It's a big flat.'

'I like space.'

She nodded. That was a sentiment she understood. She thought of her own tiny flat, which she loved, but it would fit inside this place ten times over.

'Please, sit down,' he said over his shoulder as he walked over towards the state of the art open plan kitchen and got out a couple of glasses. 'What can I get you to drink?'

'Water would be lovely, thank you,' she replied, staying resolutely standing.

He brought over her glass and she took it, careful not to make contact. 'Thanks.'

He took his own glass over to one of the oversized squashy black leather sofas and sat.

'Why didn't you want to go to the community centre with your neighbours?'

Wow — the last question she'd expected. She wondered how much she should share, strangely she wanted to tell him the truth. Self-preservation, however, made her trot out the practised response.

'I don't like crowds.'

He didn't believe her, she could see it in the suspicious glint in his eyes. She felt suddenly vulnerable, almost as though he could see into her mind and pick out the lie she'd just told.

She stared back defiantly and was hit with the realisation he might be hiding as much as she was.

Now, where had that thought sprung from?

He put his glass down on a side table. 'You had no problem with the crowd at Daisy's party.'

She downed her water and set the glass beside his. 'That's different — Daisy's party was crowded with children.'

He didn't react, but stared intently,

almost as though he were observing some sort of alien specimen. And she supposed that analogy might not be so very far from the truth; she'd put money on his not inviting clowns into his inner sanctum on a regular basis.

'Why don't you like being called Brianna?'

She exhaled in one slow breath and claimed the farthest corner of the same sofa. In the car he'd been quiet and she hadn't realised how lucky she'd been. He was far too clever, and this inquisition had completely taken her by surprise.

She wistfully thought back to the infinitely preferable quiet, brooding Nathan.

'It's daft. You'll laugh.'

'Tell me.'

She took a deep breath. Even she knew it was a silly reason, but as a child it had upset her so much. She even toyed with fabricating a response, but eventually waded in with the truth.

'When I was young, other children used to shorten it to Brian and tell me I was

really a boy — now I never use Brianna
in case I get mistaken for a man.'

★   ★   ★

Nathan's gaze skimmed over her slender
curves, the tiny waist outlined by her tight
t-shirt, to the endless legs and back to her
very lovely face. Perhaps not his type, but
definitely not a man.

He couldn't help himself — the bubble
of amusement started way down in his
abdomen and erupted into a loud and
uncontrollable laugh.

As a rule, Nathan didn't laugh, it
showed a weakness he despised and he
struggled to regain control.

'I knew you'd laugh.'

She looked so hurt he relented. 'I'm
sorry. But it's pretty ridiculous — how
could anyone mistake you for a man?'

'I'm tall.'

'You're also very pretty,' he surprised
himself by saying. But as he looked at her
stunned face he wondered how he could
ever have thought her mouth too wide,

31

she was undeniably lovely.

He watched in fascination as a slow blush spread over her pale skin, up her throat until her face glowed. It had been a long time since he'd made a woman blush.

She looked up at him, her brown eyes filled with uncertainty, before she allowed her embarrassment to get the better of her and she broke eye contact.

He wished he hadn't embarrassed her by commenting on her appearance. But a man? Seriously? The suggestion was outrageous.

'I'm going to call my neighbour, Fran,' she told him, still refusing to meet his eye. 'See what the situation is at home.' She retrieved her mobile from her bag.

He could tell by the few words she spoke that it wasn't good news. Which meant she would have to stay here a bit longer. He experienced an odd ripple of joy.

Which was ridiculous. It seemed that after knowing her only a matter of hours, the transition in his psyche could only be described as momentous. For a man who guarded his space — never encouraged visitors, never even brought a girlfriend home — he was suddenly inordinately keen to have her stay.

He raised an inquisitive eyebrow as she finished her call.

'Still no news,' she confirmed. 'Everyone's still sitting it out at the community centre.'

★　★　★

Madison sighed as she put her phone back into her bag. It had occurred to her that she should maybe leave Nathan's place and join her neighbours after all. She needed to get away. It frightened her how easily she'd confessed her lingering daft childhood worries over her name. She'd never told anyone that before. Not her Aunt Zoe. Nor even Adam, who had been her very best friend since they'd met as children.

That bright idea, though, had been thoroughly erased by the cacophony she'd overheard in the background of her phone call to Fran; angry voices arguing, tired children crying.

Crowds were all very well when they consisted of happy, laughing children — but give her an unhappy group, and it would take her back to a place she'd rather not go.

She shuddered.

Much better to stay here. Despite the disturbing way Nathan Telford made her feel when he looked at her the way he was doing now.

Agitated, she perched on the very edge of the sofa — as though ready to flee at a moment's notice. Which, to be honest, she would do, if she had anywhere to go.

Nathan, however, didn't seem to have a care in the world. He lounged back, relaxation mode fully engaged.

He was still wearing his tie, though.

Despite everything, she experienced an urge to reach out and unknot it. He needed loosening up.

She tried not to smile as she imagined

the look on his face if she tried it.

'Sounds like it could be a while before you'll get home,' he said, rudely interrupting her train of thought. 'I could make us something to eat. There are eggs in the fridge — I could make an omelette.'

Madison got the distinct impression he expected huge gratitude for making such an offer. She stifled a smile. To be fair, it was kind of him, but sadly he was going to be disappointed.

'Thank you, but I'm not hungry.'

His slow grin had her face burning. 'Of course you're not,' he muttered half under his breath.

'What's that supposed to mean?'

He shook his head, not breaking eye contact. 'It's just I get the impression nothing's ever straightforward with you.'

She might have forgiven him when he'd laughed at her career choice. She hadn't even caused a fuss when he'd laughed at the childhood scars that made her go by her family name, rather than her given one.

But he'd effectively accused her of being difficult and this was a laugh too far. She decided to be offended this time.

'I'm not being awkward. I've had a terrible day. My car broke down, I've missed an important meeting, and I've been thrown out of my home. Food is the last thing on my mind.' Face still burning, she shot to her feet, grabbing her bag as she went. 'Thank you for all your help today. I think I'd better leave now.'

'Brianna.' He caught up with her before she reached the door. 'I'm sorry. Please don't go.'

Madison paused. And then she turned to look at him. He certainly seemed sorry. And when he reached out and took her hand, linking her fingers between his own, she didn't try to stop him.

He took a step closer and suddenly, she was leaning against him.

Madison's bemused gaze clashed with electrifying blue — and by that point she couldn't have left even if she'd wanted to.

Pressed up against him, she could feel the hard lines of his muscular build, the heat of his body. The desire to kiss him reached out of nowhere and gripped her hard. She watched, breathless, as his attention shifted from her eyes to her lips.

'This is a bad idea,' he told her, his gaze fixed to her mouth.

Her heart was beating wildly. She could barely breathe. She knew he was going to kiss her — and the anticipation was driving her slowly out of her mind.

'Yes, very bad,' she croaked at last.

But she got the feeling kissing Nathan would also be fun.

He leaned in even closer.

His breath was warm as it fanned her face. Even before their lips made contact, she was left reeling and she realised she'd plunged headlong into disaster number five. She fancied the pants off a man so far removed from her world it wasn't even funny.

Even while she knew it was a bad idea, knew what had happened the last time she'd dared to date someone out of her social circle, she couldn't look away.

For a long moment, they held eye contact, only a breath apart, neither daring to move.

'Brianna ...' His voice was almost a caress and it sent shivers down her spine.

'Mmmm?'

'Your phone's ringing.'

It took her a moment to register what he was telling her.

'Oh.'

She stepped away, still maintaining eye contact and was horrified to feel herself blushing — again. She was doing that a lot today. But at least things weren't as bad as they could have been — at least she'd been prevented from kissing him and making a complete fool of herself.

'Excuse me.' She rummaged in her bag and found her phone before it stopped ringing, mercifully. 'Hello?'

'Madison, it's me, Fran,' her neighbour said. 'There's news. We can go home.'

3

A Visitor

By the next day, the whole Nathan incident seemed surreal. And by the day after that, the experience was so remote it seemed almost as though it had happened in a dream. She had to keep going over the facts to remind herself it was all true.

'They found the leak and fixed it pretty quickly in the end.' She smiled over to where Zoe sat reclined on the sofa with her feet up.

Mondays were pretty quiet in the clowning world as a rule, so she'd taken the opportunity to visit her aunt. She'd related the bare basics of Saturday's drama — though she'd tried carefully to edit out mention of a certain man.

Zoe would have read too much into it — and Madison didn't need a lecture.

'So, everything's definitely sorted?'

Zoe asked, suddenly looking pale. 'There isn't likely to be an explosion or anything?'

'They made sure of it. They wouldn't let us go home until they had. Are you feeling OK?'

'Yea, I'm fine.' Zoe gave a reassuring smile. 'You know you can stay here,' she offered. 'Just until we're sure it's safe at your place. Jimmy won't mind if you camp down on the sofa bed in his study.'

Madison was touched her aunt was so concerned. She really was very lucky to have Zoe in her life. And now Zoe was married to Jimmy, Madison knew she was doubly fortunate to have two such lovely people to count on as family.

'Really?' She laughed. 'Jimmy won't mind if I sleep amongst all his folders and files — next to his beloved computer?'

'Of course he won't.' Zoe frowned. 'But on second thoughts it might not be so comfortable for you. There's always the sofa in here ...'

'Stop worrying — I'll be fine. Honestly.' She smiled, pleased to see some colour

40

had returned to the older woman's cheeks.

'Well, the offer's there if you change your mind.'

'Thank you, I appreciate it. Now why don't you tell me about your honeymoon? Where was this surprise destination Jimmy took you? Did you have appropriate clothes?' Madison sat back and listened as Zoe became animated, sharing news of her break.

'We stayed at an upmarket hotel on the coast,' she said. 'It was glorious. We walked on the beach, spent time in the pool. And the food was just fantastic — I can't believe how much I ate.'

Madison frowned, again something niggled her. Even though it wasn't so long since she'd waved the happy couple off, her aunt looked as though she'd lost weight. And she was so thin to start with, her slender frame showed up every lost ounce.

'It's my new dress,' Zoe smiled when Madison gently pointed out she was looking slim, despite how much she'd supposedly eaten. 'Jimmy treated me

41

while we were away. Wearing black always makes you look thinner.'

Madison knew Zoe would be reluctant to say if there was something wrong. If her illness had returned, for example. She shuddered, not daring to take the thought further. She was being silly. They were over all that. Madison couldn't bear to think otherwise — it would be beyond cruel for Zoe to be ill again.

The sound of the front door opening had them both turning their heads expectantly.

'Hello, my love.' Jimmy smiled at Zoe, dropped his briefcase at the living room door and headed over to kiss his wife. 'How have you been today?'

'Fine — though I felt a bit guilty that I had the day off when you had to go to the office.' Zoe glanced cautiously over at Madison before forcing a smile. 'Jimmy, look — Madison's here.'

'Lovely to see you. Has Zoe been telling you all about our break?'

'You call my honeymoon a break one more time and you'll be making your own tea,' Zoe teased.

'I was thinking we could call for a takeaway,' he suggested. 'It will save us cooking. Madison, will you join us?'

No, she decided, it wasn't her imagination. Something was wrong with Zoe. She loved to cook and never saw it as a chore. In fact, she always said it relaxed her after a long day. So why was Jimmy wanting to save her from the exertion?

She wanted to ask outright — but fear of what the reply might be was a powerful motivator to keep quiet.

'That's really kind,' she said. 'But I'd best get going — I've got a lot to do. Maybe we can have dinner soon.'

As they said their goodbyes, Madison convinced herself that she was mistaken. Zoe couldn't possibly be ill. Not now she was finally happy and settled with Jimmy. Fate wouldn't be that cruel, surely?

★   ★   ★

Nathan was irritated. For the first time in living memory, his legendary focus eluded him. He couldn't concentrate on his work — and it was making him grumpy.

With a grimace, he logged out of his computer. This was ridiculous. No point sitting here when he wasn't at his best. He wasn't in the habit of using his time unconstructively.

'Where are you going?' his assistant, Heidi, called after him as he marched through the outer office.

'Out.'

The monosyllable hung in the air. He didn't look at her. Nonetheless, he could feel her astonishment as though it was a tangible force.

Her surprise was understanable. Nathan never acted on impulse. During the working week, his every move was planned and noted in his diary.

He knew today's unexpected outing would be a point of discussing amongst his staff for weeks to come. And, significantly for a man who did not like to be the subject of gossip, he didn't care.

'When can we expect you back?'

Heidi's voice didn't betray a glimmer of the curiosity he knew she had to be experiencing.

At the door, he turned and offered her a brief smile. 'I'll let you know.'

She was a good assistant. He didn't want to annoy her. But neither did he want to explain to her this restlessness that had plagued him since Saturday.

When he'd returned home after dropping Madison at her flat, his own place had seemed empty. He'd even wondered if he might be experiencing loneliness for the first time in his life. But it seemed ridiculous — how could he miss a woman he'd only just met?

However many times he told himself it was irrational, though, he wasn't able to shake the feeling something — or someone — was missing from his life.

'If anything urgent crops up,' he told her, relenting before he made his exit, 'I'll have my mobile with me.'

She gave a brief nod, but said no more.

He couldn't even phone Madison he realised as he watched the lights signifying the lift's descent into the underground car park. Stupid man. He'd had her to himself for the best part of five hours — and he hadn't even asked for her number.

The air in the car park was welcomingly cool on his face. He went over to his car and unlocked it, but didn't drive off at once.

Claire would have her number, of course. But did he really want his sister to know he wanted to call Madison? After all the 'suitable' women she'd thrown in his path all these years, she would find it hilarious that the woman he was interested in spending more time with was a flighty and disaster-prone clown.

Not that he was interested in Madison in a romantic sense. Of course he wasn't. But she was funny. And interesting. And a refreshing change from the women who made it obvious they were trying to charm him.

He could search for her business name on the internet. Maybe he could find her number that way. A few fruitless moments on his phone told him that wasn't the way to go.

He still felt guilty as hell that she'd missed her meeting. Even though it had not been his fault and there was nothing he could have done to prevent it. But still the feeling remained — he'd told her he'd have her back by four and he'd failed to keep that promise.

Not knowing what else to do, he found himself driving to one of his health clubs. The fact he chose the one closest to Brianna Madison's home wasn't lost on him.

Telford Ten was his newest health centre, recently acquired and brought into the fold.

As he walked over the threshold, his staff immediately broke into a flurry of agitated activity around him. 'Please carry on as normal,' he told them. The fact he trusted his employees meant he didn't need use the shock tactics of an unannounced inspection. 'I only want to look around.'

'If you're sure,' Alf, the manager, said

uncertainly. 'I'll be in my office if you need anything.'

Gradually, as he roamed the place, everyone resumed their normal routine, satisfied that the visit was social rather than managerial. And Nathan busied himself with an unofficial solo tour of the place.

As he viewed the aerobics studios, a plan began to form. This particular building was unique in his empire in that there were two studios — a hangover from the recent previous owner. The plan had been to knock the two into one large room to fit in with the scheduled classes.

The exercise timetables were common to all his centres — it was the way he liked it, neat and uniform and everyone knew where they stood.

A criminal waste of space, Alf had suggested at the last managers' meeting. He'd been keen to add another class until the refurbishment took place.

Mind made up, he knocked on Alf's door and walked in. 'I think you were right,' he told his manager as he sat down.

'Maybe we need to schedule something for that spare studio.'

Alf's face lit up. 'More aerobics classes?'

'No, not exactly.' Nathan loosened his tie and took a deep breath. 'Alf, tell me, how do you feel about clowns?'

★ ★ ★

Under her breath, Madison cursed her car. If it wasn't still in the garage being repaired, she wouldn't be able to feel her hair frizzing with every drop of rainwater than fell on her head as she made her way from her aunt's house.

Probably best to head home to change, she realised, before going to see Adam. She should be going straight there — he'd phoned when he'd returned this afternoon, keen to speak to her. But her soggy and squelching shoes reminded her with every step exactly why she needed to take the detour home.

Only moments away now, she put her head down and made a dash for it.

And she collided with a solid male chest.

'Oh, sorry.' She looked up into the deepest blue eyes and her heart gave an alarming lurch. 'Oh. It's you.'

'Hello, Madison. Still haven't got your car back?'

Nathan's voice sent shivers down her spine. She tried not to show it and took a deep breath as she stepped back. She'd never expected to see him again — yet here he was.

'It should be ready at the end of the week. They're waiting for a part.' She was positively reeling from the shock of seeing Nathan when she'd least expected — she even forgot about her wet clothes and frizzy hair. 'What are you doing here?'

'I wanted to speak to you. Do you have a minute?'

'Only a minute,' she warned, glancing at her watch. 'I have to go up and change and them I'm popping over to see Adam.'

'He's back, then?'

'Yes, he is.' She nodded, her damp hair hanging around her face, a blatant reminder of how much of a mess she was. 'What do you want, Nathan?'

He ran his fingers though his too-short blond hair, now sprinkled with rainwater. 'I was wondering if you'd had any luck yet finding a suitable property.'

She frowned — still smarting from the sting of missing out on viewing the last possibility. 'I haven't heard from him today, so I'm assuming not.'

The hint of a smile played about his lips and Madison was immediately on her guard. Had he tracked her down just to make fun of her again? She liked to be entertaining — it was her job, after all — but this was beyond a joke.

'Why don't you go and get dried off. I'll wait here and run you over to Adam's when you're ready. There's somewhere I want you to see on the way.'

'This all sounds very cryptic.' She looked at him carefully — his expression gave nothing away. Only the day before yesterday she'd believed he was pleased to be rid of her. And yet now, not only had he sought her out, but he was volunteering to act as her chauffeur once more. And he was offering to show her some mysterious

51

something. That had to be odd, surely?

'What is it you want to show me?'

'Go and get changed — you'll see soon enough.'

She turned and was half way towards her building when she realised how rude she was being. How could she leave him out on the pavement? OK, so he could go and sit in his car — which she could see only a short distance away — but that wasn't fair when he'd helped her out so much on Saturday.

She took a deep breath.

'Why don't you come up for a cup of tea while you wait?'

His grin was full-blown and left her reeling. 'OK, thanks.'

It was only as they were climbing the stairs to her tiny flat that the first twinges of doubt hit her. What would he think of her home? Space-wise, it would all fit comfortably into the vestibule of his penthouse. And it was cluttered. Not dirty, but untidy and filled with books and colourful objects — stuff.

Things that were important to her.

His frighteningly neat living space flashed through her mind and she cringed a little as they approached her door. There was no getting away from the fact that, no matter how much she liked the look of him, the differences in their living arrangements proved that they were so incompatible it wasn't true.

4

A Business Proposal

Nathan was seldom wrong in his first impressions of people and he was pleased to see his instinct hadn't let him down as far as Brianna Madison was concerned. Her flat was just as he'd expected; full of colour and clutter. Even though it was not exactly to his taste, even though it brought back uncomfortable reminders, he would have been disappointed to have found anything else.

She gave a self-conscious half smile. 'Sorry, it's a bit of a mess.'

'I've seen worse.' He nearly laughed at the incredulous expression she flashed his way before heading to the kitchen. She didn't believe him. Not that their acquaintance was going to last long enough for it to matter. Once he'd righted the wrong that had been caused by bad traffic on Saturday afternoon, he'd never have to see much of her again.

In fact, if he delegated matters to his manager, he could probably avoid her altogether.

He frowned. Why didn't that idea feel as good as it should?

She was showered and changed into fresh t-shirt and jeans by the time he'd finished his tea. 'That didn't take long.'

'That's because my hair's still wet,' she commented as she grabbed a lightweight jacket off the back of a chair.

He hadn't noticed. She'd twisted it into some sort of style and pinned it up on the top of her head. It looked fine to him. 'I can wait if you want to dry it.'

She shook her head. 'We'll be here until midnight. It takes ages even with the hairdryer. Now, are you going to tell me what this big mystery is?'

*   *   *

She wasn't happy. He could tell as much just by watching from the door as she

55

prowled around the spare aerobics studio at Telford Ten. Her displeasure was obvious in the many reflections of her lovely face in the mirrors that lined the walls.

'You don't like it?'

Her head snapped around and she frowned. 'Of course I like it. It's perfect. In fact it's so perfect I'm also cast iron sure it will be way out of my price range. My business plan doesn't allow for a swanky place like this.'

He folded his arms and leaned back against the doorframe. 'We can come to some arrangement.'

The fierce light in her brown eyes as she took several angry strides towards him made him think of some magnificent warrior queen. He wondered if the wise thing to do might be to make a run for it, but then decided to take it like a man and braced he himself for a possible collision.

She stopped barely a foot short of where he stood.

'What kind of arrangement did you have in mind?'

The clipped tone left him in no doubt she'd reached the wrong conclusion. The devil in him thought it might be amusing to play along for a while, but he knew how important this was to her — and he couldn't do it.

'Nothing immoral,' he assured her easily. 'But we can negotiate a rent that's within your budget.'

'I don't want charity. I've always paid my own way and I don't need you to take me on as some sort of underdog you're going to champion.'

She was seething, her brown eyes furious. He wondered if he'd maybe made the wrong decision here, trying to help her. But Claire had told him how much it had meant to Daisy that Madison Clown had made an appearance at the party. It wasn't fair she'd lost out as a consequence.

'It's not charity,' he reasoned. 'The studio is empty. All my health clubs run to the exactly the same timetable — it's the way I like it. And my timetable only needs one aerobics studio in each establishment.'

'Then why are there two studios here?'

He shrugged. 'This is how it was when I bought out the previous owners.'

'Surely the sensible thing to would be to run two classes simultaneously?'

'You sound like my manager.'

'Then why don't you do it?' She stood, feet apart, hands on hips, trying to stare him down. Who would have thought a clown could be so argumentative?

'It's hard to explain.'

'Try.' Still those brown eyes bored into him, furious and demanding answers.

'I like uniformity and order. Symmetry in all things. Running an extra class wouldn't fit with the way I work.'

Her frown was understandable. It was difficult for anyone to know why he preferred to work like that unless he revealed more than he was prepared to about himself.

'And running a clown school in this particular branch wouldn't be asymmetric?'

'No.' Surprisingly he meant it. 'No, it wouldn't. Because your school wouldn't be part of my organisation. You'd run it separately — take your own bookings, find your own clients, plan your own classes … It would be your business and you'd be free to run it the way you've always wanted.'

That was when he saw it — just a glimmer, but it was there, deep in those brown eyes: she was interested.

'I don't know, Nathan. I hadn't thought of something like this.'

'It's a good idea.' He paused to wonder briefly why it was so important to him that she agree. Surely he'd dealt with any obligation, real or imagined, merely by making the offer? It was up to her if she declined. He watched as she looked around the empty studio and considered the plan. 'You need premises and I have an empty studio to fill.'

'I need to get my head around this. I mean, could it really work?'

'We could do a trial? Say six months?'

She wanted to accept, he could see, but something was holding her back. She intrigued him. Was she reluctant to run her business from here because she didn't want to be beholden to him?

'There's no hidden agenda,' he assured her. 'You wouldn't even have to see me, if that's what's worrying you.'

'No.' She looked embarrassed at the speed of her own response. 'No, it isn't that. How could I not want to see you when you've been so lovely?'

He smiled — he couldn't help it. She thought he was lovely. Not many people did.

She flushed softly and he felt a protective urge to put his arms around her and hold her close.

Instead, he pushed himself away from his comfortable leaning post at the door and reached out his hand. 'Come on, let's go. I'll take you over to Adam's and we can talk on the way.'

Hesitantly, almost shyly, she reached out her own hand and his breath caught as her fingertips brushed against his palm. Her hand in his was so right.

But he refused to think of why that might be.

* * *

As they drove through the evening traffic, Madison's head was reeling. Nathan had offered her an opportunity beyond her wildest dreams. She should be happy. But she also knew that setting up her business at one of his establishments would be asking for trouble.

There was no doubt she found him off the scale attractive. And there was no doubt that he was every bit as unsuitable for her as he'd been on Saturday. Working from his leisure centre would inevitably mean there would be some contact between them. She didn't know how she felt about that.

'What are your thoughts?' he asked. She stole a quick glance. His eyes were firmly fixed on the road ahead, thankfully.

Added into the complex mix now was the zing of attraction that had travelled from her fingers, all the way down to her toes when she'd reached for his hand. It was difficult to think about work when her feet tingled still.

She sighed. He'd pulled up outside Adam's home and she was going to have to give him an answer. And, really, she'd be silly to turn him down. She was a grown-up — well able to look after herself and control her responses to a man.

'If we can come to an agreement about rent, then I think I'd like to give it a try.'

'Good.' His grin set butterflies fluttering in her tummy and left her reeling.

She found herself smiling back. Even though she knew this idea was beyond bad.

'I'd better go,' she told him. Not that she was keen to leave his company. 'Adam's waiting. Thank you for the lift, Nathan.'

Adam opened the door as she walked up the garden path. Nathan started the engine and she turned, saw him glance across, the ghost of a smile on his face, and she raised her hand in a final greeting as he drove off.

This evening had been every bit as surreal as Saturday afternoon had been. Only a couple of hours ago she had been resigned to never seeing Nathan Telford ever again. Now, thanks to him, she was about to realise a lifetime's ambition to set up her clown school. And she was going to work in luxury premises — in one of his leisure centres, no less. She should really pinch herself to make sure she wasn't dreaming.

She heard a low whistle behind her.

'Was that an Aston Martin?' The envy in Adam's voice was unmistakeable. What was it with men and cars? Admittedly, Madison was fond of her own car — but it was primarily a means of transport and a way to advertise her business rather than a love affair. And she would definitely, not in a zillion years, have envied someone else's car.

She grinned, still unable to believe how her luck had run tonight.

'I really couldn't tell you.' She shrugged and allowed herself a quick glance in the direction Nathan had driven.

Adam rolled his eyes and laughed. 'I think it was. Come on, Jen's got the kettle on.'

'What's this big news that couldn't wait?' she asked, once she was settled with a cup of tea.

Jen opened her mouth to reply, but Adam got in first. 'Oh no. Before we tell us our news, we want to know why you turned up in a luxury motor — and we want to know who was driving.'

'What?' Jen's eyes were wide.

'Madison,' Adam informed her, 'just turned up in an Aston Martin.'

'Oh no — not again. Madison, you didn't go out with another snooty rich man? Don't you remember what happened with Barry?'

'Nathan is nothing like Barry,' Madison flushed. She'd made one mistake — taken up with a man who was several rungs above her on the social ladder — and her family and friends were never going to let her forget it. She put her empty mug down on the coffee table and sighed. It really wasn't fair of them. Because of Barry, nobody trusted her to make any decisions where men were concerned.

'But you're dating him? And he's got

money?' Adam was frowning — and, although she knew it was only because he was worried about her, she was annoyed by it.

She'd learned from her mistake. And that was why she could never entertain the sizzling attraction she felt towards Nathan. They would be business acquaintances — and that was all.

'It wasn't Barry's money that was the problem.' She gave a rueful smile. It had hurt at the time, but now she realised it would never have worked. 'It was his mother.'

Barry's mother had been horrified when he'd brought home a clown. The tantrum when they'd announced their engagement would go down in history — it had been a humdinger. Madison shuddered as she recalled the shouting and the tears. The memory of that evening alone was enough to put her off a romantic inclination for life.

Not even a man like Nathan, who was so gorgeous that just thinking about him made her toes curl, couldn't persuade her otherwise.

'It wasn't a date and he isn't a boyfriend.' Her voice was assertive and she was pleased about that. She needed to put a stop to this nonsense and the sooner the better. She didn't want her closest friends thinking she was daft enough to relive her lowest point.

Briefly she explained who Nathan was and how she'd met him — and about how he was going to make her business dreams come true.

Jen's eyes narrowed. 'And what's in it for him?'

The smile froze on Madison's lips. The question hit home.

OK, so Nathan hadn't wanted to offer her a lift home and he'd made it obvious he'd only done so to please his sister. But he'd been so lovely since — running her around town after she was evacuated, taking her home to his place and letting her stay until it was safe for her to go home — and now he was helping with the clown school.

Surely nobody was that nice unless they hoped to gain some advantage from it? And she couldn't pretend the thought hadn't secretly nagged her.

She dismissed her concerns. Of course he was that nice. She immediately felt guilty that it had even crossed her mind that there might be an ulterior motive in his helping her.

'It's a business arrangement,' she explained carefully. 'He's allowing me to rent space in one of his leisure centres. It's no big thing — deals like that are made every day.'

Jen didn't look convinced — and Madison still didn't like the look of Adam's worried frown either.

'Just be careful,' Jen warned. 'I don't want to see you get hurt again.'

'You don't need to worry,' Madison smiled, touched they cared so much about her, but keen nonetheless to move on from the subject. 'I have every intention of keeping my heart in one piece. Nathan Telford's not getting anywhere near it.'

And, what was more, she was sure he wouldn't want to. The attraction was decidedly one-sided. Of that she was quite sure.

'Now, your turn,' she urged with an impatient grin. 'I've been dying to know what your news is.'

'Well, you know we went away for the weekend?' Adam began.

'Yes.'

'Oh, it was the most romantic hotel,' Jen broke in, obviously bubbling with excitement. 'It was terrific. Adam got down on his knee at dinner and …' she paused and glanced lovingly at Adam.

'And …' Madison prompted, her grin threatening to split her face in two. She knew where this was heading — She'd suspected for a while — but she needed to hear it just the same.

'He's asked me to marry him,' Jen shared with a happy smile.

Just the news she'd hoped for. Adam, her closest friend since childhood — the closest thing she had to family, apart from Zoe and Jimmy — was at last going to have the stability he'd always craved. But she reigned in her excitement, for just a moment longer.

'What did you say?' she asked, hardly daring to breathe.

Jen's smile was so bright it lit the room. 'I said yes,' she finished on a squeal.

'Ahhhhhh . . .' Madison's happy scream filled the close confines of the living room and she leapt across the coffee table to where her friends sat together on the sofa and enveloped them both in a giant hug. 'I knew it,' she cried. 'I had a feeling this was going to happen when you said you were going away.'

After the laughing and the hugging had calmed down, Adam went to the kitchen to fetch champagne and three glasses. 'To the future,' he toasted.

'To my two best friends,' Madison offered. 'May you both be as happy as you deserve.'

'There was one other thing,' Jen began a little hesitantly.

Madison looked at her expectantly. 'Yes?'

'It's going to be a small, quiet wedding, but I wondered if you'd be my bridesmaid?'

That started the screaming and the crying and the hugging all off again. 'Of course I will,' Madison eventually replied, patting at her eyes with a tissue. This was really turning into a wonderful day.

'And if you want to bring this Nathan as your plus one, we won't say a thing.' Jen was obviously in a mood to be generous. But Adam looked none too happy about the offer.

'He's a business acquaintance — I told you,' she argued. While all the while thinking there was nobody else she'd rather take. Just as a friend, of course. She really wasn't daft enough to expect anything else from a man of Nathan Telford's calibre. A man like that wouldn't look twice at someone like her.

But still, her heart did a little flutter as she thought of his very handsome face and his very blue eyes. There really wasn't any justice in the world when a man was so good-looking.

5

Moving In

The weeks passed in a blur. Before Nathan knew it, it was Brianna's moving day, and Nathan had been roped in to help.

He watched the increasingly large collection of clown paraphernalia being carried into his pristine aerobics studio and tried not to wince. Coloured balls, bright artificial flowers, costumes, boxes of make-up — it just kept coming.

It had been his idea to house the school here. He had to remind himself of that. And it was a fantastic idea. Her business plan was a good one — the idea was worthy. Passing on knowledge and teaching children and young people skills that would, in turn, give them the self-assurance to face the world was always a worthwhile endeavour.

But all this stuff....He glanced over

71

to the far wall, to the walk-in cupboard. Would it all even fit in? He couldn't see it, somehow.

She'd brought with her enough equipment for an army of clowns.

Now there was a thought. He did his best not to shudder.

'I can't believe you've managed to get all this equipment together in just three weeks,' he told her as he met her at the door and took some boxes from her.

Her smile was dazzling. 'I've wanted this for a very long time,' she reminded him. 'I knew exactly what I needed to get for the set -up. The venue was the last piece of the jigsaw. Now all I have to do is find enough children to come to my classes.'

He didn't want to tell her that finding clients — and, more importantly, persuading them to pay — was the most difficult part of any business. Not when she was on such a high about her dream coming together finally.

'Where do you want these?' He nodded to the load in his arms. 'In the cupboard with the rest?'

'Yes, please.'

Nathan spotted his reflection in the studio's mirrored wall as he carried the boxes across the studio. He was smiling. He smiled a lot around Brianna Madison. He'd noticed that before.

Perhaps that wasn't a bad thing. They were learning to be friends as well as business acquaintances — and it was good that they were getting on so well.

He carefully balanced the boxes he was carrying on the very top of a tower of other boxes. He'd have to see about getting some more shelving put in here.

He carefully patted the tower to make sure it was stable. He didn't want the whole thing toppling over — particularly as there was a real danger they might crush his favourite clown if they did fall.

'I'm so excited, Nathan — I can't wait until next week,' she told him as he emerged back into the studio.

There was a sparkle in her brown eyes and her usually broad smile was even brighter. He knew a moment of pleasure that he had played a part, however small, in making her dreams come true.

Years of planning and preparing would finally come to fruition when she hosted an open day for her clown school the following week.

Nathan was looking forward to it, too. Maybe after they had that occasion under their belt, he might be able to get back to his own work. Despite his initial plans to remain detached, Brianna Madison had proved to be quite a distraction.

'Was that the last of the delivery?' he asked.

She nodded. 'That's all I can do here for now. I need to drop by the printer and pick up the leaflets and posters.'

They walked together towards the exit.

Alf smiled as they made their way out through the reception area. The manager had made no secret he was delighted the space was going to be put to good use at last — and it showed in his wide grin as he greeted them. 'How's it going?'

'Really well,' Madison told him. 'We're all set for open day up next week.'

'Really?' Alf's eyebrows were in danger of disappearing into his hairline. 'That's very fast work.'

'I want to be up and running in time for the children breaking up for the summer holidays,' she explained. 'I'm running some week-long summer schools — I've taken some bookings already, but I need to get the word out.'

'Terrific. The increased footfall, the parents waiting in the cafe, eating and drinking … I've got a good feeling about this.' He rubbed his hands together.

Brianna shook her head. 'Do you guys ever think of anything except the bottom line?' she teased.

'No,' Nathan and Alf replied as one.

Alf feigned surprise. 'Surely profit's the only important thing when you're running a business.'

'Exactly,' Nathan agreed, grinning as he quite naturally reached for Brianna's arm and led her through the door.

Their cars were parked together.

Even though he should be used to the sight, he still got a surprise when he saw her little brightly coloured clown car next to his Aston Martin. Nothing could have demonstrated more vividly how unsuited they would be as a couple.

He raked his hand through his hair.

There it was again — the notion he couldn't rid himself of, no matter how platonic he tried to keep their dealings. Why did he keep thinking of himself and Brianna as a couple?

It was obvious they weren't compatible. However beautiful she was, however happy she made him when they spent time together, anything more personal than friendship would be a complete disaster.

And that was exactly what he told himself, every single time the thought occurred to him that it might be a good idea to ask her out.

Her eyes were large and her smile wide as she looked at him now.

'Thanks for everything, Nathan.' Her words were softly spoken and he lent towards her to make sure he didn't miss anything. 'I can't believe anyone would do all this for me.'

She turned her face so he could feel her warm breath on his skin. Then she pressed her lips against his cheek.

Her kiss was soft and barely there, but he felt the touch of her lips on his skin as keenly as though she'd branded him with her mark. He hardly dared to breathe as, with a soft sigh, she moved away and got into her car.

If she was so wrong for him, why had her kiss felt as though it belonged?

Reality quickly intruded into his thoughts as he listened, with growing disbelief, to her car spluttering and coughing. Through the windscreen, he could see her deepening frown as she tried and tried to get it started. And failed.

A sense of the familiar began to creep over him. But, where he should have been exasperated, he was suddenly elated at the thought of a few more minutes in her company.

With a barely leashed grin, he walked

around to the driver's side and opened the door. 'Sounds like it doesn't want to go anywhere.'

She turned the key again and, seeming to prove his point, the engine coughed and spluttered some more before cutting out completely.

'I don't believe this,' she muttered. Her knuckles were white as she gripped the steering wheel tightly and she suddenly looked wearier than he'd ever seen her. 'There's so little time to get the arrangements finished for next week — and I have three parties arranged for the weekend. I can't afford for my car to break down again.'

He stopped himself form stating the obvious — that this was a terrible car, that rather than being disappointed when it didn't start, she should be surprised when it did. Instead, he watched as she helplessly turned the key in the ignition one more time. When nothing happened, she gave an exasperated cry before laying her head on the steering wheel.

OK, he decided, enough was enough.

'Brianna, leave it.' He reached out and took her hand so he could draw her gently out of the car. That she leaned against him seemed natural, and he brought his arms around her.

Her body was taut with stress — telling him more clearly than words would have done, how wound up she was about the upcoming open day. However excited she was and however much she'd always wanted it, he knew from experience how terrified she must be. Not only did her life savings rest on this, but, if the venture failed, she'd have to find herself a new dream.

That was a scary prospect for anyone.

He held her tight for a moment. 'I'll take you home. We can stop by the printer on the way. And I'll call my mechanic to come and pick your car up in the morning. Until it's fixed, I'll lend you one of mine.'

She lifted her head from his shoulder and he saw her terrified glance flutter briefly over to his Aston Martin.

'I couldn't possibly drive your car,' she gasped. 'It looks like it's worth a fortune.

I'd probably break it. I'm not good with cars.'

'I have other cars,' he laughed. 'You can borrow something a little more sedate, if you'd prefer.'

'Nathan, no. It's very kind of you, but I couldn't possible allow it. You've done way too much for me already.'

'Look on it as protecting my interests,' he reasoned.

'What?'

He grinned and tightened his hold of her. 'You said yourself you need the car to do the final running around for the open day. If that doesn't go as planned, how are you going to attract customers and how are you going to pay your rent for the studio?'

She smiled and he relaxed.

'Well, if you put it like that.'

⋆　⋆　⋆

All her life Madison had relied on herself to sort everything out. OK, so maybe she'd had Zoe and Adam for emotional support as she'd grown up. But the practical stuff, well, despite her ditsy image and clown job, she'd always been quite good at that.

Now, though, she wasn't sure what had happened — she was relying on Nathan more and more. Oddly, it felt quite good to know he was there. His shoulders were broad and he was always kind and eager to help.

When he pulled up outside her flat, she was oddly reluctant to get out. She wanted to prolong this moment in his company. Just a little. Just enough so she could wrap herself in the memory and sleep a little easier, knowing he was on her side.

'Thank you, Nathan,' she told him softly.

His eyes locked on hers and his smile was achingly intimate. 'My pleasure.'

She smiled back — more reluctant than ever to let him go. 'Do you have time for a cup of tea?'

'I really must get going. I've got a dinner dance to go to later.'

'Oh.' It was daft to feel this disappointed. 'Well, have a nice time.'

'I won't,' he assured her. 'The place will be full of stuffy contacts. But I have to go — someone I hope to do business with will be there. He's about to sell his health club and I'm hoping he'll agree to sell to me.'

Madison raised an eyebrow. 'Telford Eleven?'

'Telford Eleven,' he confirmed.

She forced a smile to disguise her disappointment. 'Well, I'll let you go. Thanks again — for everything.' She got out of the car and, before closing the door, she leaned back in for a moment. 'See you tomorrow.'

'Come with me?'

She wasn't sure she'd heard right. His words had been softly spoken, just as she was about to close the door. Heart racing wildly, she leaned back in. 'Sorry?'

'The dinner — come with me.'

She shook her head in shock. In the weeks she'd known him, worked with him, he hadn't come close to asking her out. She wasn't prepared for it. Terror filled her. Partly at the prospect of dinner with Nathan, but also at the thought of all those stuffy business people he'd mentioned would be there. 'No, Nathan … I don't think....'

'Please?' he interrupted before she could finish and her heart went wild. 'I'd really appreciate the company.'

'If you need company I'm sure there are other people you can ask.'

'But I'm asking *you*.' She'd never seen his eyes darken to quite that shade of blue before and she couldn't look away.

She felt her face grow warmer and she gulped a painful gulp of air into her lungs.

'OK,' she agreed at last, even though she thought it was a terrible idea. She had no business going out with him to a dinner. But how could she refuse when he'd asked her so nicely?

'I'll pick you up in an hour. It's formal.'

His parting shot had her scampering up the pathway.

Formal? Heaven help her.

★ ★ ★

Nathan Telford in a business suit had not prepared Madison for the sight of him in a dinner jacket, his dress shirt arctic white, a black bow tied at his throat.

'Wow, you're just gorgeous,' she blurted out without thinking as he stood on her doorstop. And then she immediately hated herself for being quite so candid.

'Er, thank you.' He looked surprised and she was horrified that she might have embarrassed him. But then he smiled as he took in her appearance. 'You look pretty gorgeous yourself.'

She shifted uncomfortably beneath his gaze, but she kind of believed him. She'd experienced a brief moment of panic when she'd let herself into the flat after he'd dropped her off earlier. She didn't own many smart outfits — not these days. She'd thrown most of them out, vowing never to go to any more formal occasions after what had happened with Barry.

A night out at the local pub would do her fine in future, thank you very much — and she had plenty of informal outfits for that sort of outing.

But then Nathan has asked her out …

Thankfully she'd remembered the soft blue silk gown she'd worn as Zoe's maid of honour a few months ago. Even the silver heels she'd worn with it would do because, even though she was tall, Nathan was a good six inches taller.

The place was crowded when they arrived. They stood just inside the ballroom's doorway and looked down onto the dance floor. Glittering couples milled around, sparkling and being witty and interesting. It wasn't until her breath was expelled in one whoosh that she realised she'd been holding it.

Another moment of panic rendered her immobile as she stood next to Nathan. A small sound of distress escaped her lips. The music was too loud for him to have heard, but he must have picked up on her reluctance to go any further because he slipped his hand into hers and gave her fingers a brief, but supportive, squeeze.

'Don't worry,' he whispered in her ear. 'They don't bite.'

She so didn't want to be here — and it was a mark of how much she wanted to spend time with him that she'd agreed to come tonight.

They found their table and Nathan made the introductions. Madison was seated between Nathan and his lawyer — a lovely man who spent the meal chatting to her and making her feel at home, while Nathan discussed business with others at the table.

'Sorry I neglected you while we were eating,' he told her as they danced after the meal had been cleared away.

'Not a problem.' And it wasn't, but trying to think clearly while she was dancing in his arms was proving difficult. 'You warned me this was a business dinner. Did you secure Telford Eleven?'

'I think so.' He grinned and her tummy flipped quite alarmingly. 'You're sure you were OK?'

She nodded. 'Clive was telling me about his family. His wife couldn't come tonight because she's looking after their granddaughter while their daughter is in hospital about to have her second baby.'

She had enjoyed chatting with the lawyer, but she was out of her depth at this crowded and glamorous event. It was way more glamorous — and busy — than anything Barry had ever brought her to. And, judging by the way Nathan's arm tightened around her, it was pretty obvious he guessed how uncomfortable she was.

'Next time, I'll make sure we go somewhere that's a little quieter.'

She missed a step and pulled away so she could look at him. Next time? He was planning to take her out again? His expression gave nothing away and she wondered if she might have misheard. The band was very loud, after all.

She really hoped she hadn't. Even though she knew it would be bad for her, she quite liked the idea there might be a next time.

And, just like that, she realised she was in over her head where Nathan Telford was concerned — it was far too late to keep the relationship strictly business.

She sighed. 'I just didn't expect quite so many people, that's all.'

He guided her around the room, each step faultless.

Barry hadn't been able to dance a step, despite his mother having sent him to ballroom classes when he'd been a child. It was nice to be on the dance floor with someone who knew what he was doing.

His hand tightened on the small of her back, and he pulled her closer again, so she was leaning against him, her cheek resting against his. Yes, she was very glad she'd worn her heels.

'What I don't understand is,' he whispered into her ear, making her shiver, 'you're a performer, how can having dinner in a room with a few people worry you?'

A few people? Her gaze swept the crowd. A few hundred, more like. 'When I'm performing, I'm Madison Clown,' she reminded him. 'I hide behind my costume. Tonight, it's just me.'

'Just you is fine with me. It's nice to see you in something other than shorts or jeans or your clown costume.'

There was something about the way he said the word 'clown' that concerned her. And it wasn't the first time she'd noticed he seemed to disapprove of her career. She pulled back slightly again, far enough to see his face, and carefully tried to read his expression through narrowed eyes.

'You don't like clowns, do you?'

There it was — a hesitation so brief she might have missed it if she hadn't been looking for a reaction. Her suspicion was spot on. And, even if he quickly rushed to reassure her, she knew the truth now.

'Actually, as you ask, I don't like clowns in the least.'

OK, so no reassurance was forthcoming. At least he hadn't insulted her intelligence by lying. But it wasn't what she'd wanted to hear — even if she knew it was silly to still feel so upset. A lot of people found clowns creepy, she knew that and accepted it. And she'd never before been so tempted to burst into tears at the knowledge.

She sniffed as his hand closed over her trembling chin. He lifted her face with gentle fingers, so she was looking up into his eyes.

'I don't like clowns,' he told her again. And while his words seemed harsh, his tone was so kind she wanted to give in and dissolve into a sobbing wreck. He stroked her chin with his thumb. 'But I do like you.'

And then he brought his lips to hers in a kiss so sweet it made her want to cry for quite a different reason.

6

Preparations

Nathan opened his eyes and found Madison looking at him with a slightly confused expression. He lifted his hand from her back and ran unsteady fingers through his hair.

'I'm sorry,' he managed at last. 'I shouldn't have done that.'

Her eyes widened. 'Why not?'

He'd been over it in his head so many times since he'd met her. 'We're too different.'

'And yet a few minutes ago you were talking about us going out again.'

He sighed. He *had* said that. And the thought still appealed, but ... 'A relationship between the two of us would never work.'

She sighed and leaned against him for just a second before stepping back. 'I know. I've been telling myself the same thing since that time at your flat — when we nearly kissed.'

'So you understand where I'm coming from?'

'I do, but …'

'But what?'

She sighed again. 'But why do we have to define what we have between us? I know you don't want romance. I don't either. But why can't we just carry on being friends and see where it takes us?'

There was no denying her argument was logical. But he knew they were quickly moving beyond friendship and it was leading him into unchartered territory.

Nathan wasn't one to act spontaneously. He liked to have his time and his life planned out — he wanted to know where he was going and how he was going to get there. And who with.

These past few weeks with Brianna Madison had shown him a glimpse of how things might be if he let go occasionally. And, while there was no denying he could easily fall for her, he knew there was no prospect of a future for the two of them together. He would find it impossible to live her sort of chaotic life — however much he liked her.

He didn't know, though, how he could begin to explain to her that, although he liked her very much, he believed they would ultimately make each other miserable.

They were still standing, stranded, in the middle of a now empty dance floor. Around the periphery, guests were saying their goodbyes and leaving. He looked around, perplexed. Just how long had they been dancing? It never ceased to shock him how quickly time flew by in her company.

'Things are just about finishing up here, why don't we go? We can talk properly in the car.'

She gave a brief nod. 'OK. That's a good idea.'

They made their way out, Nathan raised a hand in farewell to people he knew along the way, but he didn't stop. Suddenly, speaking to Brianna Madison was the most urgent thing in the world. He had to tell her — before he changed his mind — that taking things further would not do either of them any good.

Once on the road, though, it wasn't as easy as it should have been to start talking.

He glanced across as he waited for a set of traffic lights to turn green. Her eyes were closed as she sat back in the passenger seat. She had to be exhausted. She'd been so busy trying to get everything ready for the clown school. He shouldn't have brought her out tonight — not when she had so much going on.

As he watched her, a gentle smile played about her lips. He was stunned by how beautiful she was. Not just pretty, but gut - wrenchingly, stunningly gorgeous. Why hadn't he noticed before?

'What?' she queried, opening one eye.

He smiled briefly and turned his attention back to the road as the traffic light turned green. 'What do you mean, 'what'?'

'You were staring at me.'

'Was I?' He tried to sound nonchalant, but his heart was beating wildly. How was he supposed to tell her that they shouldn't veer towards a romantic relationship, when she'd already caught him gazing at her with all the sophistication of a smitten schoolboy?

He heard her laugh softly, the sound sending a shiver of pleasure down his spine.

Despite everything he'd told himself, he was in so much trouble.

*　*　*

Madison knew Nathan wanted to keep their relationship strictly platonic — and she didn't blame him. She knew the arguments backwards, forwards and every way in between. They both wanted to devote their time to their respective businesses, and besides, they were just not suited to each other.

But whereas her head knew the truth, her heart felt very differently. What would be the harm in exploring what might be?

Yes, he was out of her league. Yes, she'd come a cropper the last time she'd dated a wealthy man. But Nathan was nothing like Barry.

Besides, she liked him and she knew he liked her. They enjoyed each other's company. And he'd gone above and beyond anything expected of a landlord in helping her to set up the clown school.

What was more, since they'd met, his was the first face she thought of every morning and the last one on her mind as her eyes drifted closed at night.

Even now, minutes after the event, she was suffering the after-effects of his kiss — her lips still tingled and her heart was still racing. It would be ludicrous not to explore the attraction.

It was obvious, though, by his reaction since their kiss, that he was going into retreat.

The knowledge settled into a sense of impending doom somewhere in the region of her stomach. He was going to suggest they stop seeing each other. Or, more likely, he was going to suggest they didn't start to see each other because, apart from tonight, their meetings hadn't been in the least romantic.

And even tonight had technically been a business dinner.

'I know what you're going to say,' she told him as he drove them along the brightly lit city streets.

He glanced across and his grin sent a shiver down her spine. 'What am I going to say?'

She sighed loudly, he'd made his feelings pretty clear on the dance floor. 'That we shouldn't see each other.'

He didn't deny it. 'And you disagree?'

She shrugged. 'No, I think you're spot on. There are so many reasons why we're wrong for each other.'

He was silent for a moment and Madison glanced at his profile. His mouth was set in a straight line, his jaw clenched. For a man who had just been agreed with, he didn't look wildly happy. 'Good,' he said at last. 'So we both know where we stand.'

'Not really.' She bit painfully into her lip, immediately wishing she had just let

97

things be. But her words were out there now and she risked a glance across to his hard profile.

He let out a soft sigh and glanced across before pulling the car into a side street, switching off the engine, and turning in his seat to face her.

'OK, Brianna Madison.' He reached out and took her hand. 'Tell me, what reason could possibly be good enough for us to put ourselves through the inevitable heartache of entering into a romantic relationship with each other?'

She blinked. For a bright man he was being a bit dim. 'Isn't it obvious?'

He gave an almost imperceptible shake of his head. 'Not to me.'

'Then I'll spell it out.' She took a deep breath. 'I think we should see each other because that's what we both want.' He continued to stare, his fingers burning into hers. And Madison struggled to breathe. 'It is what we both want, isn't it?'

For a moment there was silence and Madison was tempted to retract her words, but then his lazy smile made her tummy flip.

For so long after Barry she'd been worried about getting hurt and she'd kept away from romance. It was a measure of how much she liked Nathan that she was willing to trust him with her heart. Even if she was only expecting 'happy for now' rather than 'happy ever after'.

'Yes,' he agreed at last. 'Yes, it is.' He leaned forward, so she could feel his breath on her face. She tingled from head to toe as her gaze homed in on his mouth. 'It most definitely is.'

And then he brought his hand to her chin and closed the gap between them.

★   ★   ★

The days flew by. Nathan had been as good as his word and had loaned her a small hatchback, which had proved to be a lifesaver. And he'd promised to let her know when her own car would be ready.

When her phone rang while she was in the middle of preparations on the eve of her open day, Madison was sure it would be Nathan calling with news on that front.

It wasn't.

She smiled all the same when she saw the name on the display.

'Hi, Zoe.'

'Darling, how's it going?'

She looked around at the muddle of paraphernalia. 'Yea.' She smiled. 'I'm getting there. Should all be ready in time for when you all arrive. If I get a good tailwind.' She was sounding a great deal calmer and more confident than she felt — which she was glad about as she didn't want her aunt to fret.

'Erm, about that ...'

Fear gripped her. Again there was that sense of something being wrong. 'What is it, Zoe?'

'Jimmy and I won't be able to make it tomorrow, I'm afraid.'

Madison gripped the phone so tightly her knuckles turned white, almost afraid to ask. 'What do you mean you can't come to the open day?'

'I'm sorry, darling. You know there's nothing I'd like more. Unfortunately it's just not possible. Jimmy and I both have a lot on with work and … well … you know how things are.'

Madison smelled an excuse. It wasn't like Zoe not to support Madison's every effort. The nasty niggle that had been lurking at the back of her mind became a full blown siren blast of concern.

'Something's wrong,' she told Nathan when he arrived a few minutes later. She was still shaking after her aunt's phone call — so worried it wasn't true. 'I think she might be ill.'

'Did you ask her?'

'She says it's nothing — that work's horrendously busy just now.'

Nathan took the large box she'd been struggling to open, and slit it open with his keys. 'Maybe that's all it is.'

Madison shook her head. 'Normally Zoe would be here with bells on. Especially as she knows I was relying on her and Jimmy to help.' Madison took out a selection of brightly coloured clown costumes in varying colours. 'Whatever's keeping her away must be serious. I'm expecting a big crowd tomorrow — I'm really going to be struggling on my own and she knows that.'

'Maybe she realises you won't be on your own.' Nathan flashed a grin.

'She knows Adam can't make it. He can't get time off work.'

'But there will be members of my staff on standby. And Claire's mentioned she's coming — she'll be happy to help. And I'll be here, too.'

She looked up in surprise. That was the last thing she'd expected he would do. 'But you're always so busy. I can't ask you to help.'

'I've decided I'd rather be here with you, so I've cleared my schedule.'

Madison didn't know what to say. She was overwhelmed to know he was prepared to pitch in to help when she knew the open day would be the exact opposite of everything he liked. She couldn't look at him, it was all too much. Instead, she looked at the colourful balloons he'd helped her inflate yesterday, the multi-coloured bouncy balls he'd arranged, the wooden clown car he'd helped move into position so it was ready for a troupe of tiny clowns.

And she looked around at the wonderful studio he was allowing her to use for a rent that was so reasonable it was practically daylight robbery on her part ...

He'd done so much already. She should thank him for the offer and politely refuse. And, quite apart from her reluctance to impose on him, their arrangement was a casual one — where they spend time together as long as they enjoyed each other's company and it was fun. It could all end at any time. She didn't want to learn to rely on him any more than she already did, because it would only make it harder when she had to manage without him. As she inevitably would.

But, even weighing it all up and knowing what she should do, she still didn't want to tell him not to be here tomorrow. She wanted him here with her on what she hoped would be the most important day of her life. 'Really?' she croaked at last. 'You've really freed up time so you can volunteer to help out at my open day?'

He looked slightly embarrassed as he shrugged an awkward shoulder. 'You'll need as many pairs of hands as you can get. If everyone who replied turns up, you'll have two hundred children and parents here over the course of the day. You'll be demonstrating the skills you plan to teach and you can't keep order and persuade parents to sign their children up for your classes as well. You'd need to be a magician rather than a clown to manage that on your own.'

She smiled. 'Well, now you mention being a magician ...' She waved her hands and produced a colourful trick bunch of flowers seemingly from mid-air, the same way she always did at parties for the birthday girls and boys. With a flourish, she presented it to him. 'For you,' she beamed. 'For being so lovely and considerate.'

'Full of surprises, aren't you.' His fingers brushed against hers as he reached for the flowers and her entire hand tingled.

As she looked into his eyes, her smile

faded. 'Seriously, though, thank you for thinking of me and arranging to be here tomorrow. It means a lot that you'd do that.' No man had ever put himself to so much trouble for her before. Well, not unless you counted Adam which she didn't because, even though he would have done anything for her, he was more like family than anything else. 'Especially as you're scared of clowns.'

He laughed softly in response to her teasing. 'Not scared of them, exactly. Uneasy around them.' He took both her hands in his own. 'You don't have to take everything on yourself, you know.' He pulled her gently toward him and dropped the lightest of kisses on the end of her nose. She liked the gesture because it made her feel cherished and cute and all the things a man had never made her feel before.

Not even Barry.

Especially not Barry.

She nodded, squeezing his fingers gently. 'OK.' She wasn't going to question his motives or to remind him they were only supposed to be seeing where spending time together would take them. Instead she was going to accept what he offered. 'And now I know you're amenable to taking time off work, how do you feel about coming with me to a wedding a week on Friday?'

He looked a little startled and she couldn't help laughing.

'No need to be so concerned — I'm not proposing to you.' The laughter faded as she realised it wasn't funny he was so worried by even the fleeting thought of marrying her. 'It's my friend's wedding.'

Hopefully, by the time the wedding arrived, she would have had a chance to speak to Zoe to put her mind at rest and she'd be able to enjoy herself.

* * *

He released a breath he hadn't realised he'd been holding. Just for a moment there … No, never mind. It wasn't exactly that the thought of marrying her — Brianna Madison the person — terrified him, it was the very idea of the chaos and the disorder that always surrounded her that worried him.

While he was with her, Madison's vibrant personality made the chaos seem charming. But there was no way he could live like that on a permanent basis — forever. The thought terrified him. He needed order. He needed plans. He needed to know where his life was going.

If he tried very hard, he could just about imagine himself married. And, even though the face of his future wife eluded him, he knew she would be the embodiment of calm and serenity. She wouldn't have a riot of wild curly hair, or make her living in such a haphazard fashion. And she would have a calming effect on his equilibrium, rather than invading his mind even when she wasn't with him and making his heart beat erratically whenever he thought of her.

But Brianna Madison didn't ever ask for much from him. In fact, this was the first request she'd made. And it was the least he could do — she had accompanied him on a number of occasions now over the past few weeks and had made achingly dull business dinners enjoyable.

He didn't like weddings, but he could absolutely go with her to her friend's. If he was honest about it, he was actually pleased she'd asked. 'I should be able to manage that.'

Her smile made his heart beat a little faster and he found himself grinning back at her.

'Good,' she said. 'Now how about I treat you to dinner — to thank you for all your hard work?'

'I thought that's what the flowers were for.'

She smiled. 'You've been a busy boy — you deserve dinner, too.'

They went to a tiny bistro not far from Telford Ten and they were shown to a secluded corner table.

'Who's getting married?' he asked after they'd ordered.

'My friend, Adam.'

'Ah, the one whose doorstep we nearly camped out on the day we met.' Was it her imagination, or was that a fond smile on his face at the recollection?

Not knowing what else to do, she merely nodded. 'And the same one whose house you dropped me off at after showing me the studio. That weekend he was away was the one he proposed to Jen. I know it seems quick, but they didn't see any point in waiting, so they've arranged a small ceremony as quickly as possible.'

'No fuss — I approve of that.'

She laughed. 'I thought you might. Neither has any family, so it's just going to be a quiet ceremony.'

'They have no family?' As a man who had enough family to fill the Albert Hall, he found that concept odd. 'Neither of them?'

She shook her head, her toffee coloured curls bobbing around her shoulders as she did so. 'The reason Adam and I are so close is because we met in a children's home when we were nine. Neither of us had anyone else and we used to pretend we were brother and sister. Zoe was too ill to care for me at the time.'

His sharp intake of breath actually

hurt his chest. She'd had nobody else. He didn't like the sound of that — didn't like to think of her being all alone, apart from her childhood friend and an aunt who was sick. 'What happened to your parents?'

'Car crash, when I was a baby. I was in the back strapped into my baby seat — not a scratch on me. But they … well, they weren't so lucky.'

He reached across the table and squeezed her fingers, trying to imagine how hard it must have been for her. But it was impossible. He'd rebelled big time against the disorder of his childhood, but he'd been engulfed in the love of his parents and his many siblings. And that love had made him feel valued and safe. 'So Zoe raised you until she became ill?'

'She was more than happy to have me. She still feels guilty I had to go into care.' He noticed she shivered a little and her hand trembled in his. 'I was lucky,' she carried on. 'Zoe was well enough for me to go home after a year, but Adam was orphaned when he was five and spent the rest of his childhood in the home. He met Jen there the year before he left.'

'I can understand why you're so close to Adam.'

'He's the nearest thing I have to a brother.'

The waiter arrived and she pulled her hand away to make room for him to put their drinks down. She picked up her fizzy water and sipped.

'Your aunt made a full recovery?'

'She's been well for years — that's why I'm so worried now. The way she's behaving — the way Jimmy's suddenly so fussy around her — well, the only conclusion I've reached is she's suffered a relapse.'

He watched as her teeth sank into her lower lip and he loathed that there was nothing he could do to make things better for her. 'Talk to her,' Nathan advised. 'Ask her outright. You may well find she's fine and you've been worrying about nothing.'

'I hope you're right.'

★   ★   ★

111

Madison was waiting outside Telford Ten bright and early the next morning as Alf arrived and unlocked the building. 'So,' he commented. 'Big day.'

She nodded. 'Sure is — I've waited for this such a long time. I just hope it all goes to plan.'

'We're all here for you, he told her as she headed through to the clown school studio. 'Nathan's arranged some extra staff to help — and just shout if you want anything else.'

'Thank you, that's very kind.'

'Perhaps,' he grinned. 'Or maybe it's self-preservation.'

She stopped walking and turned back. 'What do you mean?'

'The boss would have me strung up if I didn't offer to help.'

'Oh.' Mortification engulfed her. 'I'm sorry. I don't mean to put you to any trouble.'

'Take no notice of me,' he grinned. 'I'm always pleased to help. Just … surprised Nathan's getting so involved.'

A warm glow spread through her as she

let herself into the studio. She'd suspected he was going out of his way to help her, but Alf's words had confirmed it. Maybe, just maybe, it was a sign he might care for her a little more than he was prepared to admit? She made a mental note to think it all through later.

For now, she had other things to occupy her mind. Getting her new business off the ground for one. Worrying about her aunt for another.

She'd barely slept last night — she was so excited about her new venture. But worry tinged her happiness — she knew Nathan was right, she couldn't put off speaking to Zoe much longer. She'd already resolved that once she'd finished here this afternoon, she'd phone to see if she could get to the bottom of what was happening.

7

Clown School

Claire arrived first, trailing an excited Daisy and a frighteningly sophisticated Adrianne. Madison resisted the urge to frown — she was delighted to see Nathan's sister and his niece, of course, but she had no recollection of extending an invitation to the other woman.

She remembered her well from Daisy's birthday party. She'd been haughty and superior and had monopolised Nathan's time.

'We wanted to see if we could help you set up,' Claire offered.

Adrianne's lip curled in apparent distaste. 'I just had to come and see what all the fuss was about, darling,' she muttered, refusing to meet Madison's gaze.

'You're very welcome, of course,'

Madison lied through her teeth with a forced smile.

'Is Nathan here?' the other woman tried to make the query sound casual as she glanced around. Suddenly it all became clear — Adrianne was no more interested in clowns than Madison herself was in nuclear fission. The other woman was here on a predatory mission to continue her campaign to ensnare Nathan.

Madison forced down a painful flash of jealously that threatened to bubble up as a hysterical shriek instructing Adrianne to leave him alone. Instead, she smiled as far as she was able. 'Not yet.' Turning away, she held out her hand to Daisy. 'I'm just about to get into my costume, do you want to come and help me?'

Madison took Daisy's hand and led her to the basket of colourful child-sized costumes that sat in the corner. 'And,' she added, 'I could really do with a helper today.'

With a squeal, Daisy broke free and delved into the costumes, finding an orange and purple one that was a perfect miniature replica of Madison's own costume.

★ ★ ★

Nathan had arrived and was standing with his sister and Adrianne when they returned, both she and Daisy fully transformed. He was looking just a tiny bit terrified as Claire's glossy friend hooked her talons into his arm.

Madison didn't like it — she wanted to rush to his rescue. She wanted to tear Adrianne's hand away and throw her out of the building. Luckily, common sense prevailed and she hid her jealous frown behind her clown's smile.

'Well, look at you.' Claire got down on her knees to admire her daughter's clown make-up and costume. 'You look just like a clown.'

Daisy giggled. 'I really want to learn to be a real clown. Can you ask Madison now please, Mummy?'

Claire smiled. 'OK, sweetie.' She turned her perfectly made-up face towards

Madison. 'We wondered if there might be space for Daisy to join one of your classes?'

Madison hadn't been expecting that. 'Of course,' she said. 'But it will be quite a journey from your place.'

Claire's smile seemed a little forced. 'Daisy, darling, can you go and see if you can find some juggling clubs for Uncle Nathan?'

Madison was so concerned at something obviously wrong she quite forgot to laugh at the thought of Nathan trying to deal with juggling clubs. They all watched as Daisy the tiny clown ran off to the other side of the room and then Claire began to speak in a low voice — keeping a careful eye on her daughter as she did so.

'Thing is, I've left Simon.' She turned to her brother. 'Nathan, you don't mind if Daisy and I move in with you, do you? I know you don't like having people round, but it's not as though you're short of space is it?'

'Of course Nathan won't mind,' Adrianne broke in, offering an opinion as though she had every right.

Madison felt Nathan shudder at her side — she didn't know if it was because of his houseguests or because of Adrianne's answering on his behalf. To his credit, though, he didn't say anything.

By then Daisy was back and the adults had to behave. Somehow, she'd managed to balance four of the juggling clubs in her tiny arms and she offered them to Nathan. Open-mouthed, Madison watched as he threw first club, then another, and another, then the fourth, in a display of juggling as perfect as she'd ever seen. Transfixed, she stood immobile as she watched the surprising sight — incapable of even speaking as the display went on and on …

She was suddenly aware of the mad curls of her wig bouncing merrily as she laughed. 'You dark horse,' she muttered and he turned and grinned, his blue eyes meeting her mirthful gaze full force.

'One of my many talents.'

Claire laughed at Madison's obvious surprised. 'Didn't he tell you? He was quite the juggler as a boy.'

'You didn't think I'd turn up to the open day of a clown school with no discernibly useful tricks up my sleeve?' Not breaking eye contact, he began to throw the clubs to Madison — she caught each one and made a swift return.

'If you can ride a unicycle, you're perfect clown material.'

And still they juggled to and fro, all the while keeping eye contact. Madison felt herself drowning in those blue eyes — if muscle memory hadn't been helping out with the juggling she wouldn't have stood a chance.

'No,' he admitted. 'My talents do not extend to unicycles.'

'Well, this is all very cosy.' Adrianne swiftly forced attention back in her own direction — and broke the spell holding Madison and Nathan.

Wincing as she dropped a club on her foot, Madison cast an exasperated glance at the other woman. This was the first insight into what made Nathan tick — not as a businessman, nor as a breathtakingly gorgeous companion, but those little habits and abilities that made a person unique. She wanted to learn more — how had he learnt to juggle? And why?

Seeing Adrianne's satisfied smirk, she decided to lay her claim. Walking over to Nathan, she took hold of his tie and pulled him along in her wake as she marched over to the costume corner.

'Brianna, what are you doing?' he sounded mildly amused.

Dragging you out of harm's way, she wanted to tell him. Instead, she took a deep breath. 'You've earned the right to some clown paraphernalia.'

★ ★ ★

She began to rummage in her box of clown clothes and Nathan wondered if the wisest thing for him to do might be to escape. If she thought he was going to dress up …

Despite the surge of pleasure he'd experienced when he'd managed to surprise her at her own game, he was beginning to wish he'd kept his juggling talent a secret.

Because it wasn't just the costume — he knew there would be inevitable questions. He could see them in her eyes. And soon he was going to have to admit where his need for routine and planning had come from. He was going to have to share with her the little boy he'd once been — so desperate for order in his world of chaos that he'd spent an entire summer teaching himself how to juggle.

'I have staff here. If I dress up like a clown I'll never live it down.' He tried to keep his tone light, but she must have picked up on something because she stopped rummaging and looked up at him, a soft smile playing about her lips.

'I wasn't really going to make you dress up like a clown.' She laughed softly. 'I can't believe you thought I'd do that.'

He threw back his head and laughed. 'You had me going there for a minute.'

They stood a short distance apart, oblivious to the others. Despite her make-up, he couldn't take his eyes from her face.

'You wouldn't have let me force you into a costume, surely?' She was still grinning. 'Against your will?'

'If you'd asked me? Of course I would have.' He wanted to gather up and kiss her thoroughly, but that would have to wait. 'So if you don't want me as a clown assistant, why did you drag me all the way over here?'

She leaned in closer. 'You want to know the truth?'

'Yes.' He was looking into laughing brown eyes, unable to look away.

She leaned in even more. 'Sure?'

She was toying with him, and he was enjoying every minute of it. 'Never been surer of anything.'

She was so close now that the curls of her clown wig brushed his face. 'I wanted to get you away from Adrianne,' she whispered.

'What's wrong with Adrianne?' He played devil's advocate. 'Claire says she's very nice.'

'I'm sure she is.' Her lips pursed momentarily, before she came back with an uncharacteristically snippy remark. 'She just hides it well.'

'What's the matter, Brianna?' Her gentle grin set his pulse racing. 'Jealous?'

Brown eyes wide with shock, she looked up at him, and he held his breath as he waited for her reply.

'Perhaps.' Again, it was barely a whisper, but it was the answer he'd wanted. He felt himself grin. 'Yes. Yes, I am.'

'You don't need to be.'

She looked up and a promise of a possible future shone in her eyes. In that moment, he wanted that future more than anything.

★   ★   ★

They came, as they'd promised — crowds of them — all eager to find out more about Madison's clown school. By late afternoon, as the event was winding up, they were all exhausted.

Adrianne had long since vanished, but

Nathan, Claire, and Daisy had stayed until the bitter end.

'I think I should maybe get Daisy back to your place,' Claire told Nathan, then she turned to Madison. 'I'm so sorry. I wish I could stay to help tidy up, but she's had a very busy day and I really think I should get settled before she gets too tired.'

'Of course you must,' Madison said. 'She's been brilliant. You all have. I don't know how would have managed without you. But I can finish up here so you lot get along.' She smiled at Nathan, his sister, and his niece.

'Oh, no,' Claire protested, 'Nathan doesn't need to come. I'm sure he'd rather stay here with you.'

'You'll be OK?' Nathan asked his sister. She nodded and he took a set of keys from his pocket and handed them over. 'I'll be there as soon as I can.'

Claire shook her head. 'Don't worry about rushing back — we'll be fine. We just need somewhere quiet to stay for a few days — I don't expect you to act as agony uncle.'

Madison was sure Claire must be putting a brave face on things. Leaving one's husband was a pretty big thing. But she didn't know Claire well enough to interfere — and Nathan didn't seem overly worried in any event.

'If you're sure, I'll see you when I see you, then,' he said to Claire. 'Help yourself to anything you need. The bedding for the spare bedrooms is in the linen cupboard, and there's plenty of food in the fridge.'

If Claire was upset at being dismissed in this manner, she didn't show it. She pecked Nathan on the cheek. 'Thanks, bro. Don't know what I'd do without you.'

'Maybe stay with one of your other siblings?' He smiled to soften the blow.

That surprised Madison, she hadn't been aware that there were any more members of the family. But then that was hardly surprising when Nathan spoke so little about himself.

She made a mental note to ask him the next time she got him alone.

With help from the staff from Telford Ten, the studio was pristine in no time, despite the number of very messy children who had attended.

'I think it went well,' Madison said when they were alone in the studio and she was wiping the make-up from her face.

'Maybe too well.'

Her head snapped around. 'What you mean by that?'

'Only that I don't know how you can expect to cope if your classes are going to be as busy as today suggests they might be. And I'm guessing you're not going to give up on your parties, not when you've worked so hard to build that side of things up.'

'Yes, I was thinking I might do some parties even when the school's established. Besides, I still have bookings for the next few weeks,' she admitted. 'I had to keep things ticking over while I looked for premises and some of the parents booked quite far in advance. I can't let them down.'

She sighed as she brushed out her hair. She'd gone through everything so many times, been so sure it would all fall into place that she hadn't worried too much about things. But the premises had come about so quickly in the end.

Nathan was right, she wasn't going to be able to do everything herself as she'd hoped.

'When I get things going properly, I'm going to have to take on staff, aren't I?'

'I'm afraid so,' Nathan agreed. 'Now why don't I treat you to dinner to celebrate today?'

She smiled. 'It went well didn't it. I'm so pleased. And so grateful to you and Claire for everything you did. But I really can't take up any more of your time. You should go to your sister, be with her. I'm sure she'll want to talk. She's left her husband for goodness' sake — she'll need to talk to someone.'

'Claire will be fine. She knows I'm no good with sympathy and shoulders to cry on.'

Madison was shocked. 'I can't believe the kind, lovely man who has been so wonderful to me is washing his hands of his sister when she must need him.' She shook her head.

'If there was nobody else, I'd try to be useful. But, in addition to Claire, I have four other sisters and a mother who are all much better equipped to deal with tears and complaints about romantic matters than I am. As soon as Daisy's in bed, Claire will be on that phone, and will have all the support she needs.'

Madison felt a little better about Nathan's sister and her situation. But, for herself, she was very sad that she would never know the comfort of five siblings — and a mother — to rely on.

'Now, how about that dinner?' Nathan reached out a hand and she took it without hesitation.

In the car park she made for the little hatchback Nathan had let her borrow. 'Any news on my car? Should I phone the garage to chase?'

'I phoned them this morning,' Nathan said. 'They're still waiting for a part. But you can keep this as long as you need.' He nodded towards the little car and she felt dreadful that yet again she seemed to be taking advantage of his good nature.

But he didn't seem to mind, and he didn't seem to be letting go of her hand either.

'We'll go in my car,' he said and she nodded, too tired to argue.

Even though the extent to which she was beginning to rely on Nathan was scaring her.

8

Happy for Now

Even though he could see Madison was tired, Nathan knew there was something that had to be done before they could settle down to eat. 'Where does your aunt live?' he asked as he started the car.

She looked across at him, all big brown eyes and his heart lurched as he saw how tired she looked. He wanted to take all her worries and her troubles away. And while he wasn't sure that he could do anything to sort this out, he knew that helping her to face the issue of what was going on with her aunt would mean she would deal with it all the sooner.

'Why do you want to know where Zoe lives?'

'You need to speak to her,' he said softly. 'And the sooner the better. If something is wrong, then the sooner you know the sooner you can help and be supportive. And if there's nothing the matter, you can stop worrying.'

Quietly, she gave him the address.

It didn't take them long to get there, but she seemed reluctant to get out of the car.

'Do you want me to come in with you?' he asked. He thought it best that she go in alone, but maybe she needed support.

She shook her head, this time the gesture was emphatic. 'Probably best you don't. I don't want to leave you out here in the car on your own, but if there is something wrong ...' She shuddered, then forced herself to smile at him. 'And there's always the fact that I haven't told them we're spending so much time together.'

'Are you ashamed of me?' he teased, trying to make her smile.

His planned worked and she grinned at him. 'Never. But it might be a bit of a shock for them to be introduced to you, and to realise how well-to-do you were all in one go.'

Well-to-do wasn't really an expression

he would have connected with himself — he was just a normal, hardworking guy. But he let it pass as she hopped from the car and headed for her aunt's doorstep, knocking lightly and waiting for just a moment before somebody came and let her in.

Nathan sat back and prepared for a bit of the wait. If it was bad news, he wanted to be here for her when she came out. Oddly, despite his failure to help Claire during her current crisis, the thought of leaving Madison alone to deal with something traumatic wasn't something he was prepared to do.

If she'd had other people to call on, as Claire had, it might be different, but she didn't. He discovered that the day he'd driven her back from Daisy's party.

He only hoped he would be useful to her if she needed emotional support. The reason he spent so much time working was that you knew where you were with facts and figures and business deals. Nathan knew from his upbringing that he was completely out of his depth when it came to anything more personal.

Madison had been inside for a quarter of an hour when he saw the door open and she appeared. There was something upbeat about her step as her long, jeans-clad legs practically skipped back to the car.

She was grinning as she slipped into the passenger seat.

'You were worrying about nothing?' There was no way she could have received bad news, not when she was looking so happy.

She nodded. 'You were right to make me speak to her. Oh Nathan, it really is the best news. Zoe didn't want to tell anyone too soon, but seeing as I was concerned about her, she told me. She's not ill — she's been suffering from morning sickness.'

'That's good news.'

'Definitely. She wasn't sure she'd be able to have children after her treatment. She said she's found it almost impossible to keep quiet, but she wanted to be sure everything was OK — given her age and everything. I should have guessed. I can't believe I was so stupid. After all she is newly married, and she's always wanted children of her own. She was lovely to me when I was young. She's going to be a wonderful mum.'

They drove along the still sunny streets, Nathan knowing exactly where he was going, and Madison not really caring, judging by her happy smile.

'What about you?' He couldn't believe he was asking her this — it was none of his business. Yet he still wanted to know the answer and pressed on regardless of how wise it was. 'Do you want children of your own?'

He could feel her gaze on him and he knew what she had to be thinking. Why was this man she was seeing on such a casual basis asking such a personal question?

Her soft sigh filled the car. 'Yes, I think so. Some day. Don't you?'

His grip tightened on the steering wheel. Why had he opened this line of questioning? Was he an idiot? The answer to that was obviously a big fat yes, he was — around Madison, at any rate.

'No, I don't.' The answer was definite. He didn't even have to think about it. Children had never featured in any of his plans for the future and he couldn't see that ever changing. Spending time with his only niece Daisy, and doubtless other nephews and nieces when they came along, was more than enough for him.

Which was even more proof, if proof were needed, that he and Madison were completely unsuited.

He glanced across in time to see her nod. 'Well, everyone's different.'

She didn't seem particularly bothered by his revelation.

'True.' He smiled as he parked the car near the restaurant.

It was still early, and they enjoyed a quiet dinner, chatting over the success of Madison's open day.

'I couldn't believe it when you started juggling.' Amused brown eyes glanced across at him.

'I'm full of surprises.'

'Are you going to tell me how you learned to do that?'

He gave into the urge to reach across the table and take her hand. She smiled and he brought her fingers up to his lips and kissed them. He'd never been one for public demonstrations of affection, but Brianna Madison was having all kinds of strange effects on his behaviour.

'You want to know all my secrets?'

She looked into his eyes and it was a connection so deep it practically took his breath away. The air between them sizzled. He never wanted to let go of her hand, but the waiter had brought their main courses, so he had no option.

In a way, he was grateful for the interruption. A few moments more of gazing into her eyes and he knew he would have told her everything.

After they'd eaten and were back in his car, the logical thing to have done would have been to take her back to Telford Ten to pick up the hatchback, but he wasn't ready for the evening to be over just yet.

It seemed much more natural to take

her back to her flat. She looked up from the passenger seat and smiled. 'I guess I'll be walking to work tomorrow.'

'I'll pick you up on my way to the office and drive you.' He silently willed her to ask him in, to issue an invitation to that very cramped and tiny flat — because, as long as she was there, there was no place he would rather be tonight.

'Can I tempt you with a cup of coffee before you go?'

She seemed to read his mind, and he wasted no time in getting them both out of the car and into her flat.

★ ★ ★

Madison couldn't move. She could barely breathe.

They stood just inside the threshold to her home, Nathan having firmly closed the door and locked it as soon as they were inside. He was now leaning back against the frame, arms folded, those intense blue eyes fixed on her face.

Despite all her fine words about

keeping things casual, about not getting serious, she'd never wanted anything more than she wanted to kiss Nathan right now.

Keeping eye contact, he slowly uncrossed his arms and reached out to bring a hand to her waist. When he pulled her against him, she didn't resist, instead she snaked her arms inside his jacket and snuggled closer.

'This isn't a wise move,' he said. Nevertheless, he closed his eyes and brought his lips to hers. His mouth worked some kind of magic and, before she knew it, she was pulling at the back of his shirt, bringing it out from his waistband, allowing her touch to meet the smooth, warm skin of his back.

'Very unwise,' she agreed as he moved his attentive lips to her eyelids, her face, her neck …

She shivered gently as he nibbled at the sensitive spot between her neck and shoulder and her hands tightened on his back, pulling him even closer.

She'd heeded the warnings. She knew

all the arguments backwards forwards and inside out. They were complete social and emotional opposites.

She ran her fingers up and down his spine and felt him shudder beneath her touch. It seemed that, physically at least, he was as keen on her as she was on him.

But just as he was wrong for her — everything she didn't need in a man — she was wrong for him. He deserved a woman who was sophisticated and serene and had a respected professional career. The inferiority complex that had been inspired by Barry's behaviour was alive and kicking and still a country mile wide in the face of her attraction to Nathan.

'You OK?' he asked against her skin.

She was incapable of answering, so she nodded. And, when he pulled her top away from the waistband of her jeans and warm fingers stroked her bare skin, she was powerless to protest.

She wanted Nathan — and no thinking sensible thoughts or warnings from friends and family would change that.

It was late by the time Nathan arrived back at his flat, but Claire was still up.

'Did you find everything you needed?' He went over to the fridge and took out two bottles of mineral water and handed one to Claire.

'Thanks.' She unscrewed the top and took a sip. 'Yes we were fine, thank you. Daisy is fast asleep in your spare bedroom.'

Nathan nodded. He didn't really feel it was his place to get involved in his sister's emotional difficulties, but at the same time he felt he should say something. 'What does Simon think about you both staying here?'

She gave a little sigh. 'I don't imagine he's too happy.'

At that moment, Nathan's mobile buzzed to life. Imagining the worst, getting a call at this time of night was never good, he glanced at the display. It was Simon.

He listened to what his brother-in-law had to say, feeling his expression slip with each word. 'I need to get back to you

140

about that,' he said as he ended the call. And he turned to his sister. 'You haven't told him where you are.'

Clare's face crumpled. 'Nathan, don't be cross. I was so unhappy in that house, and he just wouldn't listen.'

'That doesn't mean you can take off — with his child, I might add — without letting him know you're both alright.'

At least she had the good grace to look ashamed of herself. 'Thanks for not telling him we're here. I'll phone him when I've had time to think.'

'He sounded frantic. You need to ring him tonight. Now.'

'I'll do it in the morning.'

'Is there more going on here then you're telling me?' Nathan had never suspected it, but you never knew what went on behind closed doors in a marriage. 'Has he been cruel? Unkind? Unfaithful?'

Claire's appalled expression gave him the answer he needed. 'Of course not, he's a sweetheart. It's just he's never there — he's always at work here in London. He's only ever home at weekends and

141

even then he brings work home so he's distracted. There really isn't much point in being married if you never see each other, is there?'

'It takes a lot of money to keep that big house of yours going. If he doesn't work how would you pay the bills?'

'That's another thing,' Claire said, 'I'd rather downsize so we can spend more time as a family. And Daisy will be starting school soon and I'd like to get a job. But there's nothing to be had around there.'

'So what do you want to do?'

Claire's eyes lit up. 'Move to London. That way Simon would be home every night, he'd save time travelling at weekends, and I could find work to help with the bills.'

'It's not me you should be talking to.' Nathan passed his phone over. 'Ring your husband,' he told her softly. 'And do it now.'

He didn't move from where he was sitting on the sofa. It wasn't exactly that he didn't trust his sister, but he wanted to make sure she put Simon's mind at rest.

She wasn't on the phone for a long.

'He's going to come around tomorrow and we're going to talk.' She gave a loud sniff as she handed back his phone. 'Happy now?'

'He was worried, Claire.' A horrible thought flashed through his brain of how he might feel if it had been Brianna would had run off and he had no idea where she was.

She nodded. 'I know.'

'Phoning him was the right thing to do.' He forced any thoughts of Brianna away. This was about Claire and her family. 'Simon's a good man. You can't just throw your marriage away without giving him the chance to put things right.'

He saw Claire's eyes widen in surprise, as well they might. This wasn't like him — it was so unlike him he was even scaring himself.

'I think Madison's working wonders on you.'

Nathan felt his jaw clench. 'What's Madison got to do with anything?'

Claire smiled — and it was nice to see

her cheer up, even if it was because she was laughing at him. 'You would never have become so involved in my problems before you met her.'

'I would always have been worried about you and Daisy.'

'I don't doubt you would have been worried, but you would still have run a mile from talking to me about anything like this.'

He knew she was right. Since giving his favourite clown a lift home from Daisy's party, his life turned upside down.

'I think I'll turn in.' Claire got to her feet, stifling a yawn as she did so. As she reached the door she turned around and looked knowingly at him.

'What?' He suddenly got the feeling he was being accused of something, even if he couldn't quite work out what it was.

'Madison's a sweetheart, too.'

He knew that. 'What are you trying to get at?'

Claire shook her head. 'Considering you have the highest intelligence of anyone in our family, you can be really dim sometimes.'

'Sometimes you make no sense at all.'

'You're so busy trying to save my marriage, can't seem to see what's right into your nose.'

'Madison and I are friends,' he insisted, taking his and Claire's empty mineral water bottles through towards the recycling bin. 'Nothing more.'

'And does she know this?'

'She feels the same way.'

Claire was shaking her head again as she left the room.

Brianna made him happy, there was no other way to describe the feeling of joy that filled him whenever he was with her. But as to anything else?

He really couldn't see that happening.

9

Work to Do

Nathan dropped by at the crack of dawn to pick Madison up the following morning.

'I could have caught a bus,' she told him. 'I hate that I'm taking you out of your way.'

'It's my fault you didn't bring the hatchback home last night.'

She was touched that he'd made the effort, and, as she slipped into the seat beside him, she leaned over and pressed her lips against his.

'Any news on my car?' she asked, though she doubted there would be since he'd left her last night.

He shook his head. 'I'll ring them this morning.'

She sighed. She'd been so used to standing on her own two feet all these years. How could she have slipped so easily into being dependent on this man? He helped with her car, her business, and she so looked forward to every moment she spent with him …

'I'll be dropping by here later for a meeting with Alf,' he said as he stopped the car outside Telford Ten. 'So how about we have some lunch together afterwards?'

Suddenly the day seemed a lot brighter for Madison, even though she knew she had a task and a half ahead of her this morning.

She was drowning in paperwork when Nathan strolled into her studio a few hours later. She hated to admit it, but she was struggling.

'I'm going to have to take somebody on sooner rather than later,' she said, aiming a frown at the offending papers for good measure.

'Do you have anyone in mind?' Nathan pulled up a chair to Madison's makeshift desk — which was really a couple of boxes some of her supplies had arrived in.

She shook her head. 'I'll have to

advertise.' She closed her eyes to momentarily block out the horror of it all. She would have to pay wages. And be responsible for staff. 'I'd hoped not to have to worry about staff for a while yet.'

This was so not what she wanted. But she did want to realise her dream of running the clown school — and this taste of reality with the paperwork proved she needed help to manage the admin side of things.

When she opened her eyes again, his gaze was fixed on her face. Despite it all, she smiled at him. And her heart fluttered as he grinned back. 'I have no idea what I was thinking, planning to do it all myself.'

'You've managed to keep up with the paperwork for the children's entertainment side of things, so you can't be that bad at it. The trouble with the clown school is that everything has happened all at once — there was no time for a system to evolve gradually.'

'I can't even manage to organise the timetables. So many names to fit in ...'

'I might have an idea,' Nathan said as he gathered the papers together. 'Put these in a bag and bring them along.'

'You know someone who might be able to help?' Her heart dared to hope. Anyone who came with a recommendation from Nathan would no doubt be perfect — which would be a relief as, having never taken on a member of staff in her life before, the thought frightened her witless.

Even though she knew she was relying on Nathan far too much, she couldn't stop herself from doing as he'd suggested and they took her paperwork out to his car.

'Who are you thinking of?' she asked as they sped off. She couldn't stand the suspense a moment longer.

'Claire,' he said. 'She has a business degree and has worked for me in the past — before she had Daisy and moved to the country. More to the point, I happen to know she's looking for a job.'

Madison studied his profile — the straight nose, the strong jaw, the blond hair that was still too short, and her heart lurched as it always did when she looked at him. 'I suppose your entire family's made up of business tycoons?'

His smile was brief — and might even have been a grimace. 'Not so as you'd notice.'

He lapsed into silence as he negotiated the traffic.

'I couldn't pay much,' she told him as the thought occurred. 'I was thinking of employing someone without much experience and training them up.'

'Claire will more than make back for you what you pay her.'

And she believed him. Why wouldn't she? It was pretty obvious but when it came to business he knew exactly what he was talking about.

★   ★   ★

They met Simon coming out of the lift as they entered Nathan's building. He was smiling and Nathan took this as a good sign.

150

'We're talking,' he said. 'And I'm coming back later and taking both of them out to dinner.'

Claire was even more positive and she grinned at Nathan and Madison as they walked into the flat. 'Daisy and I might not be here when you get home tonight. I know Simon's flat is tiny, but the three of us can squeeze in there until we can find something a bit more suitable.'

'Has Simon agreed?' Nathan was cautious; he didn't want to be too pleased that a reconciliation was in the offing if there were still major issues to be resolved.

Claire smiled. 'He's willing to make time to listen — that's all I asked for. I know if we talk we can sort something out.'

That was the best news he could have hoped for under the circumstances and he was pleased for his sister and brother-in-law.

'Where's Daisy?' he asked, looking around.

'Watching a film in the bedroom. We thought it best she was out of the room while Simon and I were talking.' Clare frowned, seeming to take in at last that he and Madison were here at a very odd time of day. 'Did you want something? Is there anything the matter?'

'You could say that,' Madison said. 'I seem to be drowning in paperwork. Nathan suggested you might be able to help.'

Claire's eyes immediately lit up. 'Bring it on.'

Quickly Madison explained what she was trying to do. 'Immediately, I need to set up a schedule of classes. That was something I couldn't prepare until I knew exactly where the building would be and all the facilities that might be on offer.'

'Go on,' Claire said. 'Tell me about how you want to run the business.'

So she did. She told her in detail of the expanded vision that included a member of staff who would deal with the paperwork and, occasionally, help out with classes. 'Is there anything else you think I need to tell you?'

'I have only one question,' Claire said, 'can I please apply for the position?'

Madison happily handed over the bagful of names and her provisional schedule and then left Claire to it.

'I can't believe how easy that was,' she told Nathan as they drove along to the café where they'd decided to eat lunch.

'Much easier than trying to do it all yourself.'

Now the mission had been accomplished, he wondered the wisdom of involving his family with Madison's business. What would happen when their relationship fizzled out, as it was bound to do?

He quickly pushed that thought away. Things were fine between himself and Madison now — and, when they cease to be fine, they would all deal with a situation like adults. She smiled across and he felt his world tilt as it always seem to do these days whenever he was with her.

He grappled with finding a thought that would bring him back to reality. 'Your car should be ready by the weekend,' he told her eventually.

Her answering smile had his heart fluttering again. Damn it — he really was losing his grip on reality.

'That's brilliant. Thank you so much.'

He was left wondering again why such a heap of junk meant so much to her. He made a mental note to ask — when he'd thought of a less offensive way to word the question.

★ ★ ★

Claire didn't take long to prove her worth as an admin whiz. The summer school timetable was sorted with a speed that had Madison's head buzzing. And she'd made huge inroads into working on the term-time schedule. She'd also started to get in touch with the parents on Madison's contact list — as well as the ones in her own network. Not to mention setting up a website — something Nathan had advised was essential.

'Money's flowing into the business,' she declared with a satisfied grin when she dropped by to give Madison an update on Friday morning.

'But I haven't even taught a single class yet.' Madison couldn't understand it.

'Daisy, darling — I'm sure Madison won't mind if you go and play with something.'

Madison smiled. 'Why don't you go and see if you can juggle with some of those bean bags?' she said — if only to see if she took after her Uncle Nathan and could prove the juggling gene was an actual thing.

'Deposits,' Claire told her once the child was occupied. 'They all want to secure places for their children and are willing to pay for the privilege.'

'I never thought of asking for a deposit.'

'No? Well, it's just as well you have me, then. They're all quite happy to pay the balance in full at the start of the course, too. That way, your costs will be covered even if the little ones don't turn up to class for any reason.'

'Oh — I really don't think that's a good idea. I'm not in this to fleece parents.'

'It's standard practice. Daisy goes to ballet and drama — and they always invoice at the start of term. Cash flow's important — especially so when you're just starting out.'

Madison realised she'd been remiss on this part of her homework. But, even though she had worked on her business plan, her vision had been made of more than facts and figures and the important part had been hopes of happy children and brightly coloured costumes. She was beginning to think this might really work, though — that it would be a viable, profit-making business. As long as Claire was willing to help.

'If the profits are big enough, I might even be able divert funds to start a tandem scheme for less advantages youngsters.' Children like she and Adam had once been.

'That's actually not a bad idea,' Claire said. 'But I wouldn't try to fund that yourself from profits. We can secure sponsorship. We can ask Nathan to contribute for a start.'

Madison was horrified. 'I couldn't possibly do that.'

'Why not? He helps out a lot with various charities. And you seem to have him wrapped around your little finger.'

Madison was speechless — but only for a moment. 'No I haven't.'

Claire laughed. 'It's not a bad thing,' she said. 'It's actually quite sweet. I've never seen Nathan like that over a woman before.'

'We're just friends,' she told Claire.

'That's what he said.' Claire was still smiling. 'And I didn't believe *him*, either.'

★　★　★

Madison was still thinking of what Claire had said as she got ready for Adam's wedding. She was so sure she'd done a marvellous job of hiding her feelings for Nathan, but Claire had seen straight through her. She would have to try harder in future.

She was putting the final touches to her make-up when her mobile buzzed. 'It's me,' Nathan's voice sounded in her ear and she shivered. 'Are you ready?'

'Yes. I'll be down in a second.'

She had one last look around to make sure everything was as it should be, pulled the door behind her, and skipped down the stairs.

She was not prepared for the sight that greeted her: Nathan, looking scrumptious as always, with arms crossed and with his firm backside leaning nonchalantly against the bonnet of her brightly coloured little clown car.

'She's back,' she squealed as she ran towards him.

He caught her by surprise when he reached around her waist and lifted her clean off the floor. And she surprised herself by giggling. She never giggled.

'Pleased?' he asked.

She responded by throwing her arms around his neck and kissing him. 'Thank you. I was beginning to think I'd never see her again.'

'As if I'd have let that happen. I know how much this car means to you. Even if

I can't work out quite why.'

'We've been together a long time. How did you get it here?' she asked as she registered his car parked behind hers.

'The garage brought it round. It's part of the service.'

Obviously a much more upmarket establishment than she was used to dealing with. She was dreading the bill turning up.

'So,' she said, 'get in and we can go to the wedding.' His horrified expression had her laughing out loud. 'It's not that bad.'

'Of course not,' he said, setting her down, but his face didn't reflect his words.

To his credit, though, he got in. And they arrived in a lesser style than he was used to at the register office.

Madison introduced Nathan to her friends — suddenly feeling very vulnerable. What if they didn't get on? And why did it matter so much to her that they did? Whatever her feelings towards Nathan, theirs wasn't a relationship destined to last.

'Where are the other guests?' Nathan asked, looking around the empty waiting area.

Jen shrugged. 'It's just us. We only need two witnesses and as Madison said she was bringing someone, we didn't need to invite anyone else.'

As Jen smiled, Adam looked at Nathan through narrowed eyes.

Madison held her breath. Surely Adam wouldn't say anything. He wouldn't be that rude. But she also knew he was very protective of her in a big brother sort of way. Nathan might well suffer from Adam's disapproval because of the way Barry had behaved.

Nathan grinned easily, seemingly unaware of the undercurrent. Adam hesitated for a moment before offering a wary half-smile in response.

And Madison heaved a sigh at this uneasy truce.

10

Meeting the Telfords

It was the briefest wedding Nathan had ever attended. There wasn't even a celebratory meal afterwards. But he and Madison stopped off for dinner.

'They just want to be married,' Madison told him as she drove them back to her flat afterwards, through Friday night rush hour traffic. 'What's wrong with that?'

'Absolutely nothing.'

Nathan could kind of understand it. If he was ever to marry he wouldn't want a big fuss, either. Though it was unlikely he'd ever get away with that.

'Did I detect a hostile tone from your friend Adam when you introduced us?' He hadn't meant to say anything — it didn't normally bother him if people didn't like him. But this was Madison's best friend and, as such, his good opinion mattered.

He definitely wasn't going to tell her, though, that Adam had cornered him for a quiet word as she had been speaking to Jen. Hunting and shooting had not explicitly been mentioned, but the threat had been clearly implied — if Nathan upset Madison, he would be made to answer to Adam.

Madison flinched a little. 'Sorry,' she said. 'He doesn't mean anything by it. He just doesn't want me to be hurt.'

'Why does he think I'll hurt you?'

They stopped at red lights and Madison glanced across. She was looking particularly stunning — her make-up was minimal and the soft blush colour of her simple shift dress suited her.

'That's what rich men do.'

He let out a breath he hadn't even realised he'd been holding.

'It's OK,' she rushed to assure him. 'I've told them all that we're not serious.'

'Them all?'

'Well, Adam, Jen, and my aunt.'

He digested that. 'So none of them

approve of our relationship?' Why was he so offended she'd told everyone they weren't serious? Especially when he'd told his sister much the same.

'It's not personal. My last boyfriend had a privileged upbringing. The relationship ended badly.'

'A privileged upbringing?' Nathan trailed helplessly. She really had no idea at all. But maybe that was his own fault: she'd seen his flat, knew about his businesses. He always played his cards close to his chest and this time the strategy had backfired.

'Are you working tomorrow?' he asked.

'I have a party booked for three.'

They'd arrived back at her flat now, and miraculously her space was still free behind where he'd parked. She reversed expertly in.

'So you're free for the next twenty or so hours?'

'I suppose. Why?'

'There's someone I want you to meet. We'll go in my car. If we leave now I'll have you back in plenty of time for your party tomorrow.'

Maybe it was time Nathan changed. Maybe it was time he finally took a woman home to meet his family.

Madison could barely believe this was happening. She wasn't the sort of girl who was whisked away on a whim. Yet, here she was, being driven to goodness only knew where, still in the outfit she'd worn to the wedding. And she was enjoying every minute of it.

'Where are we going?'

'Wales.'

She glanced across. His profile was unflinching.

'What for?'

'You'll see.'

It seemed he wasn't prepared to say another word on the matter, so she sat back to enjoy the ride.

The next thing she knew, Nathan was kissing her awake. Sleepily, she wound her arms around his neck and kissed him back.

'Time to wake up, Sleeping Beauty,' he told her, drawing away slightly.

'What time is it?'

'Late. We're here,' he told her, flicking on the inside light and then unclipping her seatbelt.

She blinked and peered beyond the brightness of the interior of the car and into the darkness. 'Not a lot to see.'

He smiled. 'If we'd arrived a few hours earlier, there would have been lots.' He grazed her cheek with the back of his forefinger. 'This is where I grew up. Where I lived until I went off to university when I was seventeen.'

'In Wales?'

'Yes.'

'You don't sound Welsh.'

He smiled. 'I've been away a long time. Over there ...' He pointed towards the windscreen. '... are some trees. It was behind those that I taught myself to juggle.'

She wished she could have seen.

'And if you turn and look through there ...' He pointed over her shoulder and out through the back window.

She turned her head and saw a building with lights still blazing in the windows.

'They're still up, then.'

He laughed softly. 'Yes,' he said. 'It seems they are. They keep late nights.'

He must have known they would be awake, she reasoned, otherwise why would he have brought her here at this time of night?

They got out of the car and he took her hand. 'OK?' he asked, giving her fingers a quick squeeze.

She got the feeling he was more nervous than she was. Instinctively feeling he needed the support, she pressed her lips to his cheek — rough stubble grazing her lips as she did so.

She'd never known him to be anything other than clean-shaven — she was obviously dragging him down to her level of casualness. The thought made her smile, even though it probably shouldn't have done.

Her smile froze as soon as they stepped over the threshold of what turned out to be a small farmhouse. The noise, the light, the colours, all hit her square in the face and she was overwhelmed to be enveloped in hugs from a number of different directions.

'OK, everyone — let Madison breathe, please.' Seemingly aware of her discomfort, Nathan took charge and they all stepped away.

'My family,' he told her with a smile. Then he turned to the curious pairs of eyes that surveyed them. 'Everyone, this is Madison.'

She was drawn in to a small, but cosy living room and sat down beside Nathan's mother.

'He's never brought a girl home before,' she told Madison in a hushed tone.

'He's never brought *anyone* home before,' one of his four newly introduced sisters corrected. 'At all. Not even friends when we were all at school.'

Knowing that made her feel somehow special — and she smiled across at him.

As she did so, though, she noticed a

sudden tightening of his jaw, a paleness to his skin — he didn't seem to be delighted that his family were fixated on the fact he'd put on hold his need for privacy for Madison to meet his family.

She felt suddenly guilty — as though she'd pushed him into it. She didn't think she had — but there was that comment she'd made about his privileged background. It seemed he'd felt the need to put the record straight.

Even though the house was homely and comfortable, there was no doubting the fact the it was small for so many children to have been raised here. Six of them. No wonder Nathan liked his own space.

'You'll stay?' Nathan's dad asked.

'Sorry, Dad — need to get back for work.'

'Huh,' his mother said. 'You and your work.' She turned to Madison. 'He was exactly the same as a boy — always gave one hundred per cent to anything he was involved in.'

Despite being easily overwhelmed by crowds of adult strangers, Madison

168

was immediately at home with Nathan's family. They were just a normal, lovely people. If she'd had a large family herself, she would have liked it to have been exactly like this one.

They chatted into the early hours until Nathan eventually got to his feet. 'We'd better make a move,' he said, heading for the door.

They all came out to wave them off.

'Don't stay away so long next time,' his mother said as she kissed him goodbye and then hugged him tightly. Then it was Madison's turn for a hug. 'Make sure you bring him back soon.'

Madison smiled weakly. It was probably best that she didn't tell Mrs Telford that, where Nathan was concerned, she exerted zero influence.

★ ★ ★

Nathan hadn't expected to feel the way he did as he drove Madison home. He was confused — his head in turmoil. It wasn't a state he relished.

He still wasn't quite sure what had happened — what had prompted him to make the impulsive decision to take Madison to meet his parents.

Maybe it was because he'd wanted her to understand — to know that his background was more ordinary than she'd imagined. Perhaps he'd wanted her to know that they had more in common than she'd thought.

Now, though, he knew he'd opened up too much of himself. Made himself vulnerable to her in a way that he was completely uncomfortable with. And he'd given his entire family the wrong impression in the process.

'You're quiet.' She spoke into the darkness as they sped along the motorway, back towards London.

Knowing she'd have to be bright and breezy for her work later in the afternoon gave him the excuse he needed for his silence. 'I thought you'd be trying to sleep.'

'The nap I had earlier on the way there will do me until we get back. Are you tired? Do you want to stop? Or shall I take over the driving for a while?'

He was touched she was worried about him. And especially touched she'd offered to drive — particularly when he knew she was a little scared of his car.

'I don't need much sleep.'

She was quiet for a while as the car ate up the miles. It was so unlike her that he was sure she must have fallen asleep despite her assurances that she wasn't tired. But then she sighed.

'What is it, Brianna?'

'Your family is lovely,' she said eventually. 'It must have been wonderful to have grown up in such a loving home. And out in the country, too.'

He winced. He loved his family — he truly did — but he found them a little overwhelming sometimes. He'd left at the first opportunity — keen to take up his chance of a university education and then to set up his business. He seldom went home.

'They must be so proud of your achievements,' she said when he didn't speak.

'Not so as you'd notice.'

'What do you mean?'

Now it was his turn to sigh. Just how much did he want to confide in Brianna Madison? This was going to be the true test of how much she meant to him.

And he suddenly realised that he had to tell her all of it.

'I never fitted in with them, not really. I was always a bit of an outsider. The things that are important to me aren't important to them. And vice versa. We don't really understand each other — and I find it's best that I keep away most of the time.'

'Nathan Telford, I can't believe you sometimes. You had such a wonderful home and people who obviously love you very much. Yet you're willingly turning your back on it because of some daft sense of not belonging? You don't know how lucky you are. I would have given anything to have grown up with my parents. As would Adam.'

That was him told. And he felt ashamed. She was right of course, but he couldn't help the way he felt. And he knew that sharing his feelings, instead of bringing them closer together as he'd hoped, was blowing them apart.

Just as his upbringing still stifled him, her upbringing left her with insecurities. Nothing could have shown that more than her reaction just now.

'Are you sulking?' she asked after a while.

He grinned in the darkness. 'No.'

'I didn't mean to have a go at you. I shouldn't have said anything — I know how I felt in the home, so many children … so much noise.'

Maybe she did get it after all.

'But I would have loved the chance to have been with my parents.'

'I know.'

And he also knew they had to put a stop to whatever was between them — before she got hurt. He was incapable of offering her the stable family she so obviously craved. It would be unfair of him — selfish, even — to keep seeing her just because it was what he wanted.

He had to put Madison first. She'd

already been through so much with losing her parents, her aunt being ill, being put in care, then that louse she'd dated … Nathan refused to be responsible for hurting her even further.

They were on the outskirts of town now. It wouldn't take him long to drive to her place, not when the early morning traffic was so quiet.

When he pulled up into a space behind her little clown car, she didn't get out immediately and he took that as another sign. She was giving him the perfect opportunity to end things.

'Madison,' he said quietly, taking her hand. 'We need to talk.'

11

Alone Again

Even though there was nobody around to see, Madison managed to keep her smile in place until she closed the door behind her. Once she was in the privacy of her own small flat, though, she leaned back against the door and allowed herself to cry.

She'd known all along that getting involved with Nathan would be a terrible idea — she'd never expected their relationship to last. So why was pain tearing her in two when she had been expecting this?

The plan had been that she would sleep as soon as she arrived home and wake up fresh for the party she was to entertain at. She couldn't think of sleep, though — not when her heart was bruised from Nathan's rejection.

'Thank goodness for make-up,' she said to herself as she got out her pots and jars and began to cover up the worst effects of lack of sleep. Just as well she no longer had to get the bus — she wouldn't have been able to negotiate public transport in her costume and going out without camouflage would have frightened everyone.

She grimaced, then plastered it on with a generous hand, before leaving home.

After all the problems she'd had, she held her breath as she started the car — but the engine purred to life and sounded better than it ever had. She had Nathan to thank for that — his mechanic was obviously made of better stuff than the ones at the many, many garages she'd taken it to herself.

In fact, she had a lot to be grateful to him for. When he had ended things, he had promised her that her studio at Telford Ten was assured. Pride had urged her to tell him to stick it, but then she remembered, not only was this her dream, but she'd made promises to children who were excited about attending classes. Not to mention that she was now employing Claire.

This was no longer just about her. Her dream had grown arms and legs and broken into a sprint — and it had gathered others up on its way.

So, she'd had to smile sweetly and say 'thank you', even though she'd wanted to scream and shout. But she wasn't about to show herself up — or to beg and plead with him to reconsider.

Most of all, she was determined not to let him read the feelings of utter desolation that swept over her at the prospect of being without him.

Maybe Nathan's civilised veneer had rubbed off on her — maybe she'd make a smart businesswoman after all.

She tried to put it all behind her so she could concentrate on the party — and, for a few hours, Nathan was a shadowy spectre that she managed to keep at bay.

'That was wonderful,' the birthday mother told her, handing over Madison's fee. At that point, a small girl ran up.

'This is Ellie,' the woman introduced. 'My niece. My sister will be looking for an entertainer for Ellie's birthday in a few months' time — she's quite keen to have you.'

Madison looked down into big eyes and a wide smile — the child was nodding furiously.

She'd briefly toyed with the idea of not accepting any new bookings for a while, just until she had the clown school up and running. But, looking at Ellie's eager face, she knew she'd never be able to do it. Another reason to be grateful to Nathan — now she had Claire to help she didn't need to disappoint this child.

Madison gave a short nod. 'I'll look forward to hearing from your sister,' she told the birthday mum, before bestowing a mile-wide clown smile on Ellie.

She tried to go straight home, but she ended up at Telford Ten. And, even though she knew a clean break was the best thing, she couldn't help hoping Nathan might be there.

He wasn't. But Claire was.

'Simon's taken Daisy swimming,' she shared. 'So I thought I'd take the opportunity to come here and see if we could have a bit of a chat about the clown school.'

Madison could have done without this — she really didn't want to see Nathan's sister until she was feeling a little stronger about the situation. But she had no choice now as Claire was here and was eager to talk business. She had so many plans, so much to discuss, that Madison's sleep deprived head was reeling within minutes.

She managed a smile as she put her hand up to try to stop Claire's constant stream of chatter. 'Just let me get changed out of my costume first,' she said, just so she could get five minutes to get herself together.

'You look dreadful,' the other woman said as soon as Madison had wiped off her make-up.

'Gee, thanks,' Madison said. Though she didn't take offence because she knew that Claire was right.

'Nathan looks dreadful, too.' She glanced meaningfully at Madison. 'I saw him earlier. I thought he might be coming down with something, but he didn't want to talk about it.'

Madison's heart had leapt at the mention of his name — despite everything. She hated herself for that — she had no right to that kind of reaction. But when she heard he wasn't himself, she was immediately concerned.

Even if she was heart-broken — even if he was the cause of it — she didn't like to think of him unhappy.

'Did he say anything at all?' she asked, hating herself that she just couldn't leave it alone.

'Nope. But then he always plays his cards very close to his chest. Before you, we didn't even meet any of the women he dated.'

Again, Madison couldn't believe that he'd afforded her the special consideration of meeting his family. Even though she'd met Claire independently, there had been no need for him to have encouraged a friendship between them — or for him to suggest they work together. And there definitely had been no need for him to take her to meet his family in Wales.

'Mum said he took you down to meet the rest of the family last night.' Claire's tone was casual, but there was no doubting that she wanted to know more.

'He did,' she confirmed.

'She said it went well.'

'Seemed to,' Madison confirmed, conscious of the fact Nathan liked to guard his privacy — even from his family — and not wanting to cause him any embarrassment.

'So what happened?' Claire gave up any pretence of subtlety and asked straight out.

Madison shook her head. There was no way she was having this conversation. 'I met everyone, we had a cup of tea, then Nathan drove me home.' She knew she'd missed out the one bit of information that Claire would be keen to discover.

'Did you fall out?'

'No,' she said wearily — because they

181

hadn't.

All would be well if she hadn't managed to fall in love with the most unsuitable man in history. She'd prided herself on knowing exactly what she wanted out of life and yet she'd deviated from the plan — and now all she wanted was Nathan.

'You're not going to tell me, are you,' Claire eventually said as the penny dropped.

'No. Not about this, at any rate.' She smiled to soften her words. 'But tell me again about how we'd go about franchising,' she urged, vowing that this time she'd listen.

★   ★   ★

The next week was hell for Nathan. He couldn't settle to anything — the work that would at one time have offered him comfort meant nothing now. He turned up at the office every single day, as he'd always done, but the appeal had gone. He no longer got the same buzz from it.

Maybe it was time he looked for a new challenge.

'We missed you at the staff meeting this afternoon, Boss,' Alf told him over the phone on the Friday after he and Madison had broken up.

Even though it had been mere days since he'd last seen her, it had seemed like a lifetime. He had been so tempted to drop into Telford Ten — as he'd done so often since she'd taken over the second studio.

'I'm not sure I'll be able to make those meetings in future,' he said. In truth, he'd only gone to the staff meetings at Telford Ten — the other nine leisure centres had been neglected in that respect. He'd told himself at the time that it was only because this was a new centre, recently brought into the fold, but the truth was startlingly obvious; the only reason he'd been so keen to go to that particular location recently had been because he knew he'd likely bump into his favourite clown.

'No problem,' Alf assured him. 'Everything's in hand in any case.'

Nathan knew it was — Alf was a good manager, which made Nathan's self-confessed meddling even more ludicrous. Nathan should have been in his own office, or meeting with potential new contacts, not concerning himself with the day-to-day happenings at one of his centres.

It had to stop. As did the instances when he allowed to Madison to creep into his thoughts.

He and Brianna Madison were over — and it was for the best.

He had a dinner to go to that evening — a business dinner, but one that he would have asked Brianna to go with him to, if they'd still been seeing each other. There was an aching sadness in his soul as he turned up alone.

'Nathan,' he was greeted by his lawyer. 'Where's the lovely Madison this evening?'

Nathan tried not to wince. It seemed however much he'd protested he and Madison were merely friends, the rest of the world had started to see them as a couple.

'I'm on my own tonight.'

And it was then it hit him — how dull life was without her. How empty it seemed without the possibility of his heart skipping a beat as he caught a glimpse of her.

The wife of one of his business acquaintances — an old friend — asked him to dance, and he knew it would be rude to refuse, but his heart wasn't in it. 'Sorry,' he muttered as he stood on her toe for the second time.

He was never this clumsy. And he'd never been this clumsy when he'd danced with Madison.

The woman smiled. 'I think you might be missing Madison,' she said softly.

His answering smile was hesitant. 'Maybe I am.' Definitely he was. But he'd get over it.

'What happened?' she asked.

He'd known her for years and knew she was being kind, but he didn't want to discuss Madison with anyone else.

'What am I doing?' he muttered to himself. He'd been so sure that Madison wasn't his type that he'd completely missed the fact she'd crept into his heart.

And there was only one explanation for the lack of joy since he'd ended things; it had to be love.

He quickly excused himself from the dinner.

He knew suddenly what he had to do. And he wasn't going to waste a moment longer.

★ ★ ★

Madison was already in her pyjamas, watching TV, with a big bar of chocolate by her side when her doorbell rang.

It would probably be Jimmy, she thought. Zoe had taken to sending him around to make sure Madison was OK. She was touched by their concern, but would much rather be left to wallow in her own misery.

She was tempted to ignore him — but when the doorbell rang again, she knew she'd have to answer. Jimmy wouldn't dare go home without being able to report he'd seen Madison and that she hadn't yet died of her broken heart. And, with her aunt's pregnancy to consider, she knew she needed to give the reassurance that was sought.

She'd forced a smile on her face before she opened the door, but the expression froze. 'Nathan.' His name sounded like an accusation on her lip.

He stood there, looking more gorgeous than he had any right to look, while she stood in bare feet, with no make-up, her hair all over the place, and her oldest pyjamas. Typical.

'Hello, Brianna. Can I come in?'

She wanted to scream that yes, of course he could. But self-preservation kicked in just in time and she brought the door just a fraction closer, closing the gap in an almost imperceptible warning. 'Why?'

'I need to talk to you.'

12

New Beginnings

Madison didn't think they needed to talk. She didn't want to let Nathan in. She wanted to slam the door in his handsome face — and to make him go away. She wanted to be left alone.

She wasn't even started on forgetting him yet and she wasn't likely to do so if he kept turning up on her doorstep.

'We have nothing left to talk about.'

Despite her brave words, faced with him now, all she wanted to do was to throw her arms around him and hold on so tightly and never let him go.

'Please — just for a moment.'

She gave a short nod, reapplied her fake smile, and stood politely aside to let him in.

Despite Claire's comment that he was

suffering after their parting of the ways, Madison could see no sign of it as she showed him into the living room. He looked the same as he always had. Strong, healthy and in charge. He was dressed for a black tie event and she guessed he hadn't made that extra effort for her. He must be on his way home from a night out — which explained why he'd called by so late.

'Is it something to do with the clown school?' she asked, not able to think of any other reason why he might be here after what he'd said the last time she'd seen him. 'Is there a problem with the studio?'

He shook his head. 'This is about us, Brianna.'

'You said enough about us last time.'

'I made a mistake. I knew it as soon as I drove off and left you, but it's taken me until now to know what I want to do about it.'

She suppressed a shudder. He was speaking as though he was discussing

189

a business deal. She could detect no emotion behind his words.

'And what do you want to do about it?'

He sighed and ran his fingers through his hair. For a moment, she thought he might show some kind of feeling, but instead he turned cool blue eyes towards her.

'I want us to go back to the way we were before.'

The words hit her a stinging slap across the face.

Back where they were before — enjoying each other's company without promise or expectation. And without hope for the future.

This was what she'd hoped for and feared in equal measure. She'd missed him so much and she could barely believe he was sitting so close by now. Yet, she really didn't want to go back to the casual arrangement they'd shared before. She wanted more — and she knew more something he'd never be able to offer her.

She shook her head.

'Is that a 'no'?' He was disbelieving. Of

course he was — he was quite a catch, after all, and he knew it.

'It's a no.'

'Am I allowed to ask why?'

She lifted her feet onto the sofa and hugged her knees. 'I can't do it, Nathan. I can't go through this again. We both knew we shouldn't have started anything — as you said all along, we're wrong for each other.'

'I've missed you.'

She closed her eyes. So not what she wanted to hear. Maybe, if he'd started with those words it might have made a difference. But not now, not when she was trying to be strong.

Her instinct told her to reciprocate. To tell him that she'd missed him, too. She opened her eyes again, to see that he'd moved closer. She forced herself to stay quiet.

His expression softened as his eyes fixed on her mouth. If he kissed her she'd be lost. But instead, his gaze lifted — and she felt the jolt of cold eyes meeting hers as he spoke. 'Is that your last word on the matter?'

Businesslike to the last.

She bit her lip. Surely Nathan on any basis was better than no Nathan at all. Was she setting herself up by making a decision she was going to regret?

But then she remembered how carelessly he'd ended things between them. She'd been devastated. And he'd walked away without a single care in the world. A relationship where one party was so much more invested than the other was never a good idea.

'It is,' she confirmed as she got to her feet. 'I'm sorry, Nathan, but I think it would be best if you went.'

He didn't say a word; he just got up and walked quietly to the door. And out of her life.

For a long time she just sat there. She wanted to go after him so much, but she didn't. And it was a long time before she could face getting up from the sofa.

★   ★   ★

Madison knew she'd done the right thing in sending Nathan away. That didn't stop it hurting, though. Or stop her hoping for a glimpse of him whenever she was at Telford Ten over the following week.

Despite being on hyper-alert, she was disappointed. He seemed to be keeping away — just as he had the previous week.

Maybe that wasn't a bad thing. The more she saw of him, the more she might be tempted to go back to the casual kind of relationship he obviously wanted — and that would be no good for either of them

No, she was glad she hadn't seen him since that night at her flat. And she was glad she'd sent him away.

Most of all she was glad that he'd ended things when he had.

Who knew what would have become of her if things had been allowed to carry on.

★　★　★

Madison's refusal to entertain Nathan's suggestion shook him. Even a week later, he didn't know what to do.

193

Not that he blamed her. He'd treated her pretty shabbily in the end.

He knew she loved him back, though, because that could be the only explanation for why her bounce had left her. She'd been pale and subdued when he'd gone to see her. And while on some level he was glad she missed him, he also knew it was his fault she was unhappy and he hated himself for it.

When he'd ended things between them, he'd truly believed that was what was best. She'd made it clear she yearned for the family life she'd missed out on growing up. He hadn't thought he would ever be able to give her that.

But he'd changed. She had changed him. He now realised there were many things more important than work. Which was why he was driving around town on a Friday afternoon, skirting around Telford Ten, wondering if she was at her studio and wondering if he should go in and find out.

Any sensible businessman would have stayed safely in his office, sitting behind his desk. But he'd discovered already he was nowhere near sensible where Brianna Madison was concerned.

It was a pity he hadn't realised until it was too late exactly what she meant to him.

He couldn't believe he'd allowed his world to be turned on its head by a clown. And he couldn't believe he'd been so stupid as to push her away.

The car was nearing Telford Ten now, but he forced himself to keep driving. He needed to put her out of his mind and concentrate on his work. And he'd start right now by giving some of his other establishments a little of attention. He hadn't been to Telford One in months . . .

The loud blast of a horn had him turning his head in horror, to see a lorry hurtling towards him.

The driver must have driven straight through a 'give way' sign. With speedy reflexes, Nathan prepared to take evasive action.

★　★　★

Telford Ten was quickly becoming Madison's second home. Between them, she and Claire had set up the first of their after-school classes — and things were hectic.

There was still no sign of Nathan as she went about the place — and she hated herself for hoping she'd see him. She was supposed to be a fiercely independent businesswoman who didn't need a man. So why was she pining after him like a lost soul.

She laughed to herself — the answer to that was blatantly obvious. Despite everything — all the warnings she'd issued to herself — she'd managed to fall completely in love with him.

She hated herself for that — she'd always prided herself on having more self-respect.

'That was a good class,' Claire congratulated her as the children filed out to be picked up by their parents.

She managed a smile. 'I think everyone enjoyed it.'

'I should say they did.' Claire looked

around. 'They made a huge mess, though. Will I sort out the costumes?'

'That would be fab — thank you.'

Before Claire could make a start, her mobile buzzed and she darted across the studio to retrieve it from her bag.

Madison busied herself with tidying up, only half listening as she picked up bean bags and popped them into the basket where she stored them.

'Nathan?' she heard Claire say and her ears immediately tuned in. 'Is he hurt?' As Claire sank to the floor, Madison went over to join her — and she strained, and failed, to make out what the voice at the other end was saying.

She didn't like the sound of this. The room seemed to spin about her as she tried not to think the worst.

'What is it?' she asked as Claire ended the call.

'You may want to sit down for this,' Claire said, pale beneath her tan.

'I don't understand …'

'That was Nathan's assistant,' Claire said as Madison sank to the floor. 'He's been in an accident.'

Even though she was sitting down, the room began to spin around even faster than before. 'What?' she managed to ask eventually.

'He's at the hospital.'

Madison nodded slowly — somehow, the information was processing in her stunned brain. She knew she needed to get to him as quickly as possible.

★   ★   ★

They turned up to find Nathan sitting in the waiting room, checking emails on his phone.

He got to his feet when he saw them.

'What are you two doing here?'

Madison didn't know if she should hug him or to hit him. All the way over here, she'd feared what they'd find — and Nathan was just the same as always. Though he did look tired — and maybe he'd lost a bit of weight, too.

'We heard you'd been in an accident,' Claire said, throwing her arms around

198

him. 'We thought you were hurt.'

He disentangled himself from his sister's hug and smiled.

'I'm touched you both rushed to my bedside, but, as you can see, I'm fine.'

'But Heidi said …'

Nathan's eyes narrowed.

'What exactly did she say?'

'She said there'd been an accident and you'd left her a message to say you were at the hospital. She couldn't come herself because her childminder needed the afternoon off.'

He gave a brief nod. 'She misunderstood. There was an accident, but it's nothing serious. Sandy — my manager from Telford One — fell off some step ladders when she was putting up poster in the centre. She said she was fine, but she was limping, so I brought her in to have her ankle looked at. I only phoned Heidi to let her know because I wouldn't be back before she left for the evening.'

'Oh.' the noise escaped from Madison and brought laser-sharp blue eyes focusing in on her face.

'So you came rushing because you thought I was hurt?' His voice was soft — his tone wrapping her up in a warm, fuzzy feeling.

'Yes.' She didn't even think to deny it.

She was aware of Claire looking from one to the other, before the other woman took a few steps back. 'I think I'll go and see about finding us some tea while we wait to find out how Sandy is.'

'My sister can be remarkably perceptive sometimes,' he told Madison, a glimmer of humour curving his lips. 'Don't look at me like that,' he warned.

'Like what?' Madison could remember what those lips had felt like on her own — and she longed to kiss him again.

The relief of finding out he was OK was making her tremble — and kissing him would be a link to reality.

'Like you want to kiss me,' he said.

She smiled. 'What if I do?'

'Ah, Brianna — you pick your moments, don't you. This is neither the time nor the place.

She knew he was speaking the truth, but still she couldn't look away. Seeing him again proved one thing — she loved him beyond anything. She loved him enough to take the risk of him hurting her again.

'When will be the time?'

She heard the sharp intake of breath. 'Are you free this evening?'

She nodded as she was aware of a woman — Sandy she presumed — hobbling towards them.

'I'll pick you up from your place at eight,' he said. And she nodded again.

$$\star \quad \star \quad \star$$

Nathan was outside her place way too early. He looked at his watch — half past seven. He knew he shouldn't, but he couldn't bear to wait a moment longer, so he took the stairs two at a time and knocked at her door.

It had been a heck of a day between everything. His lack of concentration, his near miss with the lorry, then Sandy's accident ... But it was seeing Brianna that had affected him most.

Seeing her had brought all sorts of emotions to the surface. He knew he couldn't let her go without a fight. And he was also gladdened by her pale complexion when she'd arrived at the hospital and her relieved sigh when she'd discovered he was OK.

Surely those things meant his feelings were reciprocated?

She took ages to answer the door and, when she did, he could see why. She'd obviously been in the shower — her hair was tied up in a towel, a robe hastily tied around her body. He could see the soft skin of a shoulder where the material had slipped and he longed to reach out and brush it with his fingers.

But he no longer had the right to do that.

'You're early,' she accused. But she didn't look angry.

'Sorry.'

She smiled. 'Come in while I get dressed and do something with my hair.'

He followed her into the tiny kitchen,

where she pointed at the kettle. 'Make yourself a coffee, I won't be long.'

But before she could leave the room, he reached out, touched her fingers with his own. And suddenly she was in his arms and they were kissing as though they'd never been apart.

She kissed him with warmth and passion and generosity. And, as they drew slightly apart, his arms still around her, he knew.

'You love me,' he said quietly. 'There's no way you could kiss me like that if you didn't.'

She nodded so vigorously that the towel fell from her head and her hair was suddenly in damp spirals about her face. 'Yes. But love doesn't always conquer all. You said yourself that we're too different. Our differences will come between us and drive us apart.'

She finished on a sob.

'You know that's not true. Our differences complement each other. And, quite apart from that, we have something important in common.'

She snuggled a little closer, her body language completely at odds with her words.

'What might that be?'

'Love.'

The word hung in the air between them. When she looked at him the truth was shining in her eyes.

'We can make it work,' he insisted. 'My life's been hell without you. I want to marry you, have children with you, grow old with you. I'll do everything I can to make you happy for the rest of our lives. That is if you'll let me?'

He waited for her reply. The silence seemed to last forever. He knew she felt the same way he did, but after she'd sent him away last time he wasn't prepared to take anything for granted.

'Yes,' she said.

Finally, he let out the breath he'd been holding — and she kissed him again.

We do hope that you have enjoyed reading this large print book.

Did you know that all of our titles are available for purchase?

We publish a wide range of high quality large print books including:
Romances, Mysteries, Classics
General Fiction
Non Fiction and Westerns

Special interest titles available in large print are:
The Little Oxford Dictionary
Music Book, Song Book
Hymn Book, Service Book

Also available from us courtesy of Oxford University Press:
Young Readers' Dictionary
(large print edition)
Young Readers' Thesaurus
(large print edition)

For further information or a free brochure, please contact us at:
Ulverscroft Large Print Books Ltd.,
The Green, Bradgate Road, Anstey,
Leicester, LE7 7FU, England.
Tel: (00 44) **0116 236 4325**
Fax: (00 44) **0116 234 0205**

*Other titles in the
Linford Romance Library:*

LOVE IN A MIST

Margaret Mounsdon

Minnie Hyde — flame-haired beauty and acclaimed actress of her day — leaves a legacy of confusion when she dies without a will. Penny Graham, a single parent running a pet-grooming parlour in a disused theatre on the land, is soon threatened with eviction by Minnie's grandson, Roger Oakes. That is, until long-lost Australian granddaughter Sarah Deeds also lays claim to the estate. Amidst the confusion, Penny must deal with her growing feelings for a man who would make her homeless . . .

THE DANCE OF LOVE

Jean Robinson

Starting a new phase in her life after the death of her chronically ill mother, Carrie decides to go on a cruise to Alaska. All the other passengers seem to be in couples, though, and she immediately feels left out. Then she meets fellow lone passenger Tom, who becomes a firm friend — until the handsome and elusive Greg steals her heart. Should Carrie take a chance on him, or accept the security offered by Tom? And what will happen when the cruise comes to an end?

SHEARWATER COVE

Sheila Spencer-Smith

When her cousin asks for help with running his holiday business in the Isles of Scilly, Lucy Cameron is happy to oblige. On the ferry there, she meets Matt Henderson, an attractive local marine biologist — but is appalled by his work. Soon the sea air, soft sands, and friendly locals make Lucy feel welcome; and as she gets to know Matt, she's tempted to see him in a better light. Lucy's stay at Polwhenna is temporary, though — and as the time to go home creeps closer, she is increasingly torn . . .

ROSES FOR ROBINA

Eileen Knowles

Brett had been the love of Robna's
life — until he disappeared without
a word. But now he's back in Little
Prestbury, to attend his brother's
funeral and take on the running of
the family estate. And Robbie has to
work with him . . . How will her
boyfriend Richard react — and how
will she cope? Despite telling anyone
who'll listen — herself included
— that she's over Brett, Robina just
can't seem to stop thinking about
him . . .

A LOVE DENIED

Louise Armstrong

1815: Felix, Earl of Chando, sets out to engage a suitable companion for his much-loved mother. He finds her in Miss Phoebe Allen, whose charm and good nature win him over. Once at Elwood, Phoebe also takes on the muddled household accounts, and advises Felix on how he can save the ailing estate. Felix finds himself falling in love with her — but he is determined never to marry, as he fears there is bad blood in his family. Will Phoebe change his mind?